BURNING WORLDS

GEORGIE W BIRD

tellwell

Tellwell Talent
www.tellwell.ca

ISBN
978-0-2288-1445-0 (Hardcover)
978-0-2288-1444-3 (Paperback)
978-0-2288-1446-7 (eBook)

Dedicated to Mr. Green.
Who pushed and pushed and *pushed*
me to write. No one was more
encouraging.

PROLOGUE

I set the last fork in place, to the left, on the large festive table. Pinecones and cranberry candles adorned the massive oak table equipped with fake snow and no shortage of glitter. My favourite part of Christmas was not the decorations but having my whole family gathered together for an entire day. My six siblings laughed and goofed off; we were a tight knit group. Living in a small town forced you to get along with those that were in close proximity because *everyone* was in close proximity.

All day we'd been snacking on Christmas treats that my mom and eldest sister, Sage, had slaved over and now the turkey was ready to be carved. My father always held the honour.

I was the youngest in the group at the startling age of twenty, but that didn't stop me from joining in the fun. Sure, I got teased more than my other two sisters, but that only added to my glee.

We were sitting digesting the delicious wine and savoury turkey when the lights went out and a terrible pain engulfed my entire body until the black abyss swiftly captured me.

I awoke to my eldest brother, Tyler, softly patting my hand and calling my name. Bleary-eyed and more than a little dizzy, I sat up. Chaos reigned around us. My brother was covered in blood and was as white as a sheet. The roof of the dining room was gone and a deafening roar split the air. Tyler's eyes glazed over as he whispered my name one last time.

Tears threatened to spill but I was in danger. Every fibre in my body knew it so I somehow found my legs and scrambled into the kitchen calling for everyone as I went. "Mom? Dad! Lynn? Thomas..." My breathe caught and I sank to my knees at the sight before me. So much blood...

I could barely comprehend what was happening when what could only be called a monster jumped out of nowhere and charged me. It was the size of a large dog with several eyes, two bone-like horns and a massive gnarled tail. It suddenly stopped and inhaled deeply, as if smelling me, then promptly struck my side with its massive claws. I slammed into the wall blacking out.

Hours later I stumbled out of the house in a daze. Everyone was gone. I'd searched the whole place but only bloodstains remained.

More monsters were ravaging homes in the distance and people lay dead in the street. It was a massacre. Where had they come from?

A truck swerved around the corner and skidded to a stop in front of my house. The last man on Earth I ever wanted to see came bounding out. Without a word he grabbed me into a fierce hug.

"I'm so glad you're alive."

Instinctively I pulled away. "Me too." And I knew I meant it. It no longer seemed to matter that he was a cheating scumbag, he still didn't deserve to die and it was nice to see someone I knew was alive.

"Come on," I said, "let's get somewhere safe. You got any guns?"

Luke stared at me then at the house. "Where is your family?" He didn't have anyone and when we'd been together, my family accepted him as one of our own. I didn't say anything but glared through watery eyes, daring him to press.

"Oh." His eyes widened. "You're bleeding."

I ripped my shirt and made a makeshift bandage then hopped in the truck. I barely felt the pain; I was out for blood now.

CHAPTER ONE

I sat up on my hard, green cot, panting and sweating. The dream was always the same but even after a year of recalling that horrific day, I woke up in a terror. The scars on my side ached from reliving the two-horn's so-called mercy. The first creatures to descend after worldwide blackouts were two-horns. They were the size of dogs with six black beady eyes and two massive bone horns jutting out of their skull. These Ares, as they called themselves, were without remorse or fear.

Grabbing my water bottle, I chugged down the remaining contents. Today we'd leave our cave, canvas the town for survivors, and replenish supplies before continuing south to the safe camp. In a little over a year, more than a quarter of Earth's population was dead or presumed dead. Luke and I stuck together since that first day despite our dramatic history and had picked up strays along the way. Initially we'd headed north to less populated areas to heal and try and grasp the situation.

"Breakfast!" Harriet called from the campfire.

Samuel had seen night guards lurking the night before, so we thought it best to camp deep in the forest in a secluded cave. The Ares didn't like nature. They preferred cities, almost like they'd been programmed to know that was where the humans were. The cave also helped mask our body heat against night guards, nasty beasts the size of horses with a whipping tail and deadly speed. They were blind, which made it easier to hide unless they read your body heat and were upon you before you even realized it. And worse, no bullet or blade could pierce their skin. Poor Tom, we'd lost him to a night guard only three months ago.

"The next town we hit after this one will be Calhoon," Luke suddenly said, fiddling with a knife in his hands and not meeting my gaze.

"I know," I said evenly. I felt my irritation rising. I knew we were near our hometown, how could I not? It had been more than a year since I'd left and for many months, I'd been sidestepping it. But my conscience told me there could be survivors and it was our job to help them.

"Will you be able to handle it?"

I tossed a full water bottle at him. "Yes."

Expressionless, I went to join Harriet. Her blonde wispy hair hung around her face and she smiled brightly upon seeing me walk up.

"Don't you miss milk? I miss milk. Or rather I miss having milk in my cereal. Too much milk makes me gassy."

Harriet was a morning person. I was not.

"I see. And what is making you think of milk?"

"The lack of it I guess."

She was our cook and everyday she seemed to make mention of one more food item she missed having. She was the first survivor we'd found and to our luck, she was a great cook despite her young age.

Samuel and Karl walked lazily into camp, their guns slung over their shoulders.

"No day crawlers so far. City looks safe to travel," Karl was saying.

I nodded. Day crawlers were the most terrifying to encounter. They were the size of houses with eyes that leaked poisonous tears. They only attacked in daylight, were slow, and always attacked in pairs. If we encountered one, we hid, as there was no killing a day crawler. Bullets were completely ineffective and its sheer size was weapon enough.

"After breakfast we'll head out. We need gas and food supplies."

"And maybe a shower," suggested Luke.

I shrugged. "If we find running water."

I ate in silence. I enjoyed watching Karl and Luke banter. Samuel didn't say much either, but that was usual, while Harriet never seemed to stop talking.

After breakfast, we cleaned up camp and headed out in the trucks. Samuel drove in one with me while Harry and the boys were in the other. Samuel and I enjoyed the silence together.

The town was familiar. My grandparents used to live here but had passed on many years ago, long before the invasion. Several houses were burnt to a crisp or just completely levelled. Everything was still, not even a bird chirped overhead. Cars lay deserted in the street and an eerie quiet had settled over the place. Perhaps the birds felt they weren't allowed to sing much as I felt the need to whisper when we talked.

Samuel and I drove slowly through the streets, searching and calling out for people, while Harriet and the guys went to search for food in stores and houses. It was tedious work but well worth the time and effort when helping. Samuel stopped for gas and we continued on our way.

We came to a less populated part of town thick with trees. It was harder for us to see ahead, but it would also be less likely to see any two-horns.

"There." Samuel pointed and revved the engine.

I readied my gun and took aim. A two-horn was chasing a man down through the streets, nipping his heels. The man veered left and I lost my clear shot. Samuel took cue and ripped through a backyard; they would now run right at us. I rushed out of the truck and yelled at the stranger. He headed for us but tripped and the two-horn was on him. I shot four times. Down went the beast.

"It's alright!" I called.

He couldn't seem to roll away from the alien fast enough.

"Thank you so much," he said when he finally caught his breath. "Evan Johnson's the name." His Scottish accent was as thick as his red beard. I guessed him to be about twenty-four or twenty-five. "I was searchin' for food in that cabin when he popped outta the basement. Used all ma' bullets on him but guess ma' aim wasn't true."

"Jane, but you can call me Jay."

Introductions were made, the gun was retrieved, and by the time we made it back onto the main street, Evan was a part of our little band.

"This was ma' home since I was fifteen. I hid out in these woods up by ma' ski lodge. Very difficult to get to but I just run outta supplies. Figure now's a good time as any to try an' make a real stand."

I nodded.

"Are you the leader then?" Evan asked turning to Samuel.

He shook his head and pointed at me. "No. Jay is."

Evan was startled. "But lass, you're so young!"

Before I could defend myself, Samuel gave him a fierce look, silencing Evan. "This girly saved all our lives. Including yours just now. She earned the right to be our leader."

I'd never heard the old man talk so much but felt pleasure at his warm comments and genuinely smiled.

The rendezvous point was the old church in the south end of town, as it had an easy escape route. Samuel and I checked to make sure it was empty before settling in. Harriet, Luke, and Karl arrived shortly after.

"It'll be night soon. We have to hurry. We'll head back to our cave and drive straight through tomorrow, deal?"

Everyone nodded and I spared no time in introducing Evan. Karl instantly liked him, I could tell, but Luke seemed hesitant.

"Bit of a flirt, isn't he?" he said nonchalantly. But his words sounded practiced to me.

I shrugged and watched Harriet talking excitedly with Evan. "Harry's just like that. Besides, she has a thing for Karl."

"Karl?" Luke sputtered. I knew his ego imagined Harriet had liked him and not his best friend.

"Yes." I reiterated. "Is that a problem?"

Luke's frown uplifted into an irritating smirk. "No. Of course not. Your heart is the only one I wish to capture." His flare for the dramatics were getting old and I rolled my eyes, decidedly not in a teasing way.

"Uh huh," I said none too convincingly.

"Why don't you believe me? Haven't I apologized only every other day and told you you're the only one for me?" He caught my hand and held it to his chest.

I reclaimed it with disdain. I was done playing this game. "Luke, I don't doubt you want me. But I am literally – *literally* – the only available female to you on the *planet* right now. I have no doubts that once we reach the safe camp, you'll meet many other willing ladies."

Luke sighed and I might've believed his frustration was real were it not for his previous track record. "Why won't you forgive me?"

I sighed. "I feel no malice towards you. Honestly. But I am not stupid enough to make the same mistake twice. Now go eat."

As we separated, I heard Evan questioning the status of our relationship. Harriet bit her lip and gave me a worried look. I threw her a half smile and she dove into our tragic tale.

After dinner Evan sat by me on a log. "Why do you stay with such a hateful man?"

I laughed dryly. "He is the only guy I know from back then. All our friends are gone and now we have no family. A familiar face was still friendlier than any strangers."

"But you're not together?" He tested the word as if treading on ice.

"No. Never again. He cheated on me. A guy like that can't be trusted in love." I fiddled with my fork. "It's a cruel twist of fate that brought us together."

Evan grunted. "You don't think it's weird in that crisis he came looking to make sure you, of all people, were okay? Wouldn't you say that makes you special to him?"

I laughed mirthlessly. "He didn't come find me for hours. I was the last friend he came searching for. Trust me, I was not a top priority. I was a desperate plea at best that at least someone he knew was still alive. I have tried my best to put it behind us. This is bigger than all that." I gestured to the surrounding forest to further my point.

Evan frowned at Luke from across the fire but he was too engrossed in conversation to notice. "Still, what kinda man is unfaithful like that?"

A question I'd asked myself a million times over. Unfortunately, the only answer I'd come up with was just as heartbreaking. "A dissatisfied one."

CHAPTER TWO

Taking down camp and leaving the city proved to be a smooth ride. No aliens attacked or were even noticed, probably due to the lack of humans.

The day was brightly lit without a cloud to be seen. It was early June; summer was coming. I breathed in deeply and smiled at that peculiar scent of dew and mud. It reminded me of when we went camping when I was a kid. My sisters always marvelled at how sharp my nose was. I blinked rapidly to stop the sudden tears. When would the pain end?

Karl and Harriet didn't notice my distress, they were too fond of their own company to even notice my presence in the truck.

Evan, Luke, and Samuel drove together. Evan mentioned the night before that he wanted to make sure he was in Samuel's good graces and Luke always gave me space after 'confessing' again. It gave time for his ego to reflate, much to my chagrin. The man never let up!

I scanned the tree line for anything suspicious but there were just leaves and wood. How would it feel to be in Calhoon again? We'd reach it by mid-afternoon. That left us enough time to scan for any Ares and find a safe spot to camp for the night.

For now, I felt completely calm but even imagining the town limits made my heart race. I yearned for Samuel; the fifty-odd-year-old man would understand. When we'd returned to his hometown. he'd just cried and held my hand until it bruised. I'd never seen him cry before then or ever since, but I knew he'd seen terrible things, as we all had.

The scenery never changed. Trees and more trees were all we could see as the Sun slunk across the sky. I nervously tapped the window, playing a little ditty at time wore on. I was anxious. I didn't want to see it. I could easily tell the others to take an alternative route but that wasn't fair to Luke. On the other hand, I also felt a powerful draw to return. How silly to want to go back to the place where they were slain. Nothing was there, not even graves. But somehow, I knew I needed to see it. Alone.

The "Welcome to Calhoon" sign was bent on the end and a few trees beside it were completely crushed. Entering town before scouting was foolish, so we parked the trucks inside the brush and I sent everyone in groups of two to see if any Ares were in the area before we found a suitable place to camp.

An hour later, we regrouped with an all-clear. Luke and Samuel had killed a small pack of two-horns but other than that, the city seemed safe. I was buzzing with anticipation but didn't know what I was expecting. Closure?

"The forest to the east is thick with a tight ravine. Anything bigger than a two-horn won't even be able to enter. We'll set up there.'

The Sun was waning in the sky as we rode solemnly through town. It was small, only one or two of everything essential. The grocery store was completely gone; so much for more supplies. We passed what used to be a park, where now only a single tree stood. My companions were quietly watching me, expecting me to cry, but I couldn't. There were no tears left to shed.

When the trucks finally halted, I could see Luke had been crying. He'd always been a softy. Evan and Samuel understood but still seemed uncomfortable with this sudden display of emotion. I walked up to him and pulled him into a tight hug. Dropping his gear, he returned the hug, a sob heaving his chest.

"We passed…" he choked.

"I know," I quietly said.

We'd passed his friend's house. They had been like brothers since running in diapers, especially after Luke's parents had passed.

The group was completely silent and still, remembering the dead. Finally, I patted him on the back, told him to take a minute, then meet us at the bottom. The rest of us hiked down with all our gear. It had been a troublesome day. The usual back and forth was missing and everyone looked glum. How could I liven up the night?

"I know what you're scheming, but it's all fer naught."

I whipped my head up. "What?"

Evan stood before me, tall as an oak. "Everyone in the group feels the pain you and Luke bear. We all share it.

We've all lost someone an' seen horror no person should see. So, don't be fixin' to change things."

I frowned. It was not often someone read me so well. Even my family had had trouble. "Why do you think I'm planning something?"

"You got this look ma' mum did when she was fixin' to do somethin'. A peculiar girl that one."

I smiled. "I was actually trying to plan out tomorrow… There's something I need to do."

He glanced at me out of the corner of his eye. "Oh?"

I nodded. "I'll fill you all in tomorrow. Goodnight, Evan."

He grunted as he left my lonely spot. I turned in for the night only to be met with the same sleep-robbing dream.

The Sun hadn't begun its ascent when my eyes opened, stubbornly refusing to close. What now? I sat up and gazed over the slumbering group. Harriet would probably be up in a bit to prepare food. I could help her. I knew of some berries to pick halfway up the side of the ravine. Thomas and Gideon had taken me here many times when we were young. We loved hiking and covering the walls of the rock with chalk, pretending we were cave people.

A bittersweet sense of nostalgia swept over me. It was encouraging because it didn't happen often. Perhaps soon I could think of my family with fondness and love, remembering all the things we shared instead of focusing on their horrific demise.

A twig snapped overhead and I held my breath. Slowly, I eased closer to the stone until I was flush with the wall. Listening, I waited, straining to hear the faintest noise. Nothing. I persisted in waiting a long time before collecting berries once more. I threw them into my sack until it weighed heavily against my shoulders and returned to camp.

Sure enough, Harriet was slaving over the fire, desperately trying to be quiet. "Jay! Good morning. You're up early. Ooh! Berries!"

Ugh. So, chipper. I nodded and gave her my best smile.

"What's the plan for today?" she smiled at me expectantly.

"I… I have an errand I need to run, actually. I was thinking of borrowing a car and going with Samuel while you and the others take the trucks and do the usual."

She looked at me with squinty eyes. "Where are you going?"

I scuffed my toes on a rock and popped a berry in my mouth. There was no point in lying, and no real reason to… It was just personal. "You know where, Harry."

She smiled sadly. "Ah. I tried to return home once, but my apartment building burned to the ground. Are you sure you don't want company, like moral support? Maybe Luke?"

I scoffed. "Luke is the last man I want moral support from." He'd ask questions and want to follow me inside.

"Ouch. That stings." Luke stood behind me and I could hear the smile in his voice. But it was a fake smile.

Harriet plastered on her brightest grin and greeted him warmly. "I vote today we take it slow and shower!"

"You can't wait a day? I hear lots of good things about the safe camp."

"But wouldn't it be nice to show up fresh and clean?"

I rubbed my eyebrow. "It doesn't really matter to me. Anyways, Harry, you know today's routine, fill everyone in. Sam! You're with me. I want to get an early start." I grabbed my gear as I went.

"But what about breakfast?" called Harriet.

"I had some berries!" I joked.

Samuel was ready in a jiffy and we walked into town looking for a vehicle. He didn't ask questions which suited me but I guessed he knew where we were heading and why.

"Which way?"

I pointed. "South. It's at the edge of the city, which was why I thought a car might be beneficial instead of hiking the whole way."

He agreed and we found a van parked in someone's laneway.

As we drove in silence, old memories flooded my brain. Driving this way home from school ever since I could remember, playing grounders in that park, getting Slurpees on a hot summer's day at that seven-eleven. It was both nostalgic and painful at the same time. It seemed eons ago now that I'd done those sorts of lazy things.

My heart rate increased as we neared my block and my breathing became shallow. One might think I was facing a day crawler. The van eased to a stop and I stared at my lap. Samuel said nothing and when I glanced up at him, he was busy admiring the overgrown lawns and budding trees, completely minding his own business. His salt and pepper hair made him look older. Again, I was grateful I'd brought him.

I clenched my hands into fists and slowly forced myself to look up at my house.

CHAPTER THREE

I don't know what I was expecting, but the house was oddly normal. Exactly how I remembered it, with perhaps a little wear and tear in the garden, and then there was that gaping hole in the roof. I let out a sigh of relief I hadn't realized I'd been holding. Looping the gun around my back, I opened the door and stepped out into the cool air. There was no wind and not a sound could be heard except my feet as they crunched along the gravel path and the swishing of overgrown grass. My hand shook as I opened the door and the same creak that I'd heard a million times before met my ears. Home.

Or what was left of it.

I peeked into the dining room. Big mistake. Plates and Christmas decorations were strewn about. Some chairs were smashed and the table was missing two legs. A huge stain remained where Tyler had bled out. Thinking it tightened my chest and tears stung my nose and eyes. I let them come this time.

Bracing myself, I entered the kitchen. There was stains covering everything. The floor, walls, and ceiling were practically painted in what I knew was dried blood. I walked into the center of the room and sat down listening.

The house creaked and the silence was deafening as my tears flowed faster. This place was the mingling center of our home. My sister, Sage, would bake cookies as Lynn and I did our homework and we'd chat. Music would be playing which was often interrupted by my father who insisted on old organ music or bagpipes. It didn't matter to him that our music was on the speaker, he'd turn on his phone full blast and play it anyway. I almost smiled at the memory.

Gideon and Ryan used to force me to the ground and drag me around the kitchen and I could never understand why they never did it to Lynn. Mom used to say it was because I was the dramatic one.

I don't know how long I sat there remembering those people who meant so much. I knew I couldn't remember them as that last Christmas, bloody and mangled. It needed to be the good times or I'd go insane with guilt and sorrow. It never made sense why that two-horn didn't kill me and eat my remains as well.

When my knees and butt began to hurt and go numb, I scrambled to my feet. Taking one long last look in the kitchen before heading upstairs, I left feeling a heaviness lift just from leaving the scene. Death's fingerprint was smeared all over my kitchen's walls and floors.

I sat in everyone's room, slowly taking it all in. Snooping through everyone's stuff reminded me of more fun times. Each room reflected my parents and siblings. Looking through their belongings brought a torrent of memories. My mother's gold heart necklace that I used to joke she should give me in her will; it wasn't so funny now. Gideon's ridiculous earrings. My parents had been furious when he'd gotten his ears pierced and even more so when he'd dropped three hundred dollars on ruby earrings. 'They're the new diamonds,' he'd insisted. Ryan's room had been above the living room and was barely intact. I looked under what used to be his bed and tucked behind some books and blankets, was a leather strap he often tied around his wrist.

Lastly, I went into Lynn's room. It was untouched and her bed was a mess as always. Books, clothes, and paint supplies sat in piles in her room. 'Controlled chaos,' she'd say. 'Oxymoron,' I'd reply.

It didn't take long to find what I was after: her diary. It'd wanted to read this massive private blog of her life since I was eleven years old. Finally, I'd know the truth behind every unanswered question and dirty little secret.

I sat in her room for an especially long time. It was different here. Animals hadn't gotten through the basement door and she had been my best friend. When I was young, my schoolmates insisted my sister couldn't be my friend, let alone my best friend. When I'd informed Lynn, she huffed and said that was just plain silly. I smiled thinking back which then brought another onslaught of tears.

Feeling terribly sad and lonely, I wandered into the living room. All my favourite people were gone. Everything in the room remained the same. Bookshelves filled with books lined one wall; my mother had been an avid reader. The other was filled with knives and weapons of all kinds; spears, axes, daggers, and swords littered the wall.

Suddenly I knew one other thing I wanted to take, something sentimental and practical. My father had bought daggers for each of us once we were born. My mother always rolled her eyes but he'd been giddied to get them engraved and different in their own way as a gift to himself for becoming a dad... Several times over.

I slid Tyler's and Sage's in my boots. Rummaging through an old drawer in my room, I found some belts and looping one around my thigh, I slipped on Thomas, Gideon, and Ryan's daggers. Lynn's was very small; we used to tease her about it, but my father said that was because she was premature and therefore very small, but still strong. I folded it into my pants pocket on my other thigh. I glanced at mine, but the old axe that belonged to a great-great-great-grandfather hundreds of years ago caught my eye. My father had been particularly proud of that specimen, as it was very hard to acquire. The family crest was engraved on the hilt and it was the length of my forearm, with gold plating that was very tarnished, despite excessive polishing.

The moment I picked it up to examine it, an electrifying jolt sprang up my arm and the axe clunked on the floor. Rubbing my arm, I bent to pick it up but was astonished to see the axe was gleaming like it was brand new.

"What the..." I muttered as I tested the blade.

It was sharp... But it shouldn't have been. These pieces were strictly for show. I had planned to sharpen them later... On that note I checked the daggers I'd just deposited on my person and sure enough, each blade was sharp enough to draw blood at the slightest touch.

Puzzled, I slung the axe over my shoulder with another belt and ran to my room. My eyes momentarily dry, I threw some necessities like deodorant, underwear, toothpaste, and some breathable clothes, into an empty backpack. Giving one last look into my room, I shut all the doors and headed outside.

The sun was high in the sky by the time I stepped outside, gently shutting the door behind me. For ever, I hoped. The day was just as still and quiet as before and I didn't feel all that different other than tired from such a long cry.

Just as I was stepping into the car, our trucks pulled up.

Harriet and Karl were yelling frantically and pointing at the hill behind us. The ground shook and I didn't have to turn to know. We were confronted with the biggest day crawler I'd ever seen. Dread and fear cramped my stomach. Samuel was already shooting and I too wasted no time. It wasn't long before I emptied my mag. The day crawler merely roared in anger and crushed a house across the street like it was nothing. It continued making its way toward us. If I waited to reload Samuel would be a squished bug. And where was the other one lurking? The bullets were barely effective in slowing the beast. Instinctively I drew my axe from its belt and swung. It heated in my hands and to my surprise, and that of everyone else's, a wide sweeping glowing arc spread forth from my axe. It sliced its arm off in one succinct blow. I stumbled forward and dropped the axe. The day crawler flailed and uttered a strange sound. The twin counterpart burst around the corner, trapping us in the street.

"Run!" I yelled.

My friends tumbled out of the trucks and ran toward the woods nearby, cutting over fences and through backyards. Samuel stayed put reloading; he would never run from me.

"Pick up that axe and strike again!" ordered Samuel.

Righting myself, I reached for the axe but the alien stomped on it. I only just jumped out of the way in time.

The double was coming up the rear now. Luckily, it was more preoccupied with us than my friends rushing up the wooded hillside.

"Remember, we only have to kill one!" I called as I ran to the truck. Samuel nodded and focused his bullets on the injured day crawler. It was a waste of bullets. Completely unperturbed, the Ares stomped forward. With ease it crushed a deserted car in the street. Samuel backed behind the truck but the twin was on us. We separated to be harder targets. Samuel was across the street now but the uninjured Ares swatted him and he flew across the yard landing on his back. Desperately peaking over the car, I saw him slowly roll over, groaning in pain. Relief flooded my system. He was still alive. The injured Ares screamed at me and tried to stomp on me. Almost without thinking, I whipped out Thomas and Sage and threw them with accurate precision at the incoming alien. A blue arc pushed from behind the daggers and they increased in speed. The blades pierced its eyes glazing them in poisonous bodily fluids. Both day crawlers dropped with a ground-rumbling thud.

We regrouped and stood there, too dazed to move. The shock of what had just transpired weighed upon us heavily. What had just happened? Slowly, I retrieved my axe and went searching for my precious blades. They were on the ground behind the monster and when I went to examine them, the blood and poison slid off like a repellent slime. I took a chance picking it up but found the blade was completely clean as before.

"Samuel, have you seen anything like this?"

He looked at my startled, scared face for a long while. "No," he finally admitted.

I slid my weapons back into place, shaking all over. "And thank you... For not leaving me," I said quietly.

He smiled broadly like a kid given a gold star. I'd never seen him look so childlike. "Never."

We had never killed a day crawler pair... Ever. Whenever we encountered them, we immediately retreated. It didn't take long for people to figure out and spread the word – day crawler twins were unkillable.

The rest of our group came running up. "You... You killed it!" sputtered Luke.

Harriet nodded, vigorously pointing. "We watched from the top of the hill."

I nodded, still not even certain what happened. It was like my weapons had minds of their own, directing my steps. I was a mere puppet watching it unfold. But it felt good, almost like a small win in my ultimate plot of revenge against these mindless killing machines. Finally, I could kill them right back.

CHAPTER FOUR

It was tedious work, making our way south towards the safe camp. Each day grew warmer as we tirelessly filled our time with tearing down and setting up camp, canvasing cities, and driving, driving, driving. But with my new weapons, we were less frightened of the Ares.

Luke continued to give me space and I drove mostly with Evan and Harriet. Sometimes the driving felt fun and normal, like we were a bunch of friends on a summer road trip; but then we'd pass through a town and witness the Ares' cruel handiwork and reality would settle upon us once more.

"Why do you think they're here?" asked Harriet, a question that often unsettled me. "Doesn't it seem weird that they just came to kill us?"

"Source of food?" offered Evan.

"Maybe. But only two-horns eat us. I have never seen night guards or day crawlers eat anyone, or anything for that matter. And why come to a planet filled with… with nature when it's basically their weakness?"

Those were puzzling questions I didn't like to dwell on, so I let Evan and Harriet alone in the front seat to debate amongst themselves while I filled my time staring longingly out the window. I used to love hiking but now it was too dangerous to go by myself.

"And what about Jay's blades? She basically has, like, superpowers!"

Evan looked at me through the rear-view mirror. "I have heard of people changin' after the first attack."

I perked up. "Changing?" I repeated. "How?"

Evan rubbed his thumb over the steering wheel not meeting my gaze. "That first pulse of energy that took out the power. Some people were killed by it like ma' brother. Most people didn't even notice it an' then there is a group who felt it. An' I heard it was incredibly painful."

My eyes widened. "You mean you guys didn't feel that burst of energy? It felt like my insides were doing the disco. I passed out it hurt so much."

Harriet looked at me thoughtfully, a hint of worry lining her young eyes. "I didn't feel a thing. Maybe people like you will change the tide of the war."

Glancing at the sharp axe beside me I pondered her words. What a big responsibility, to win the war.

Safe camp was deep in the redwood forest in California. The thick foliage and rutted path almost forced my group to abandon our trucks but then we were picked up by an escort who helped us the rest of the way.

I was amazed by the camp's sophistication. The base was built into the side of a cliff and surrounded by massive redwood trees. The place seemed dead until we were let into the massive bay doors.

"Orientation and bunk assignments are held over there."

The burly mustached man pointed to a check-in desk and we thanked him before making our way to the desk.

An older woman greeted us with surprise. "Well, bless my soul! You are the first refugees in months. This is so exciting! My name is Holly, come, come, fill out these forms. We try our best to keep track of everyone here and give useful job placements."

"Job placements?" asked Luke.

"Of course." She opened the office behind her and we'd barely sat before she delved into the history of the base and what sorts of job placements we could have. "We have many sections you can enter. Combat, where you will be sent on rescue missions and to kill Ares. Science, where we research and dissect the Ares. Kitchen, making meals for the masses. Maintenance, keeping the base clean and making sure that everything is running in tip top shape, and leadership. Leadership is very difficult but in the long run could be very rewarding. They run the base and communicate with the main safe camp in Mexico."

All of us stared at her.

"Are you saying you're expecting this war to carry on?" asked Harriet, who always spoke her mind.

Holly stuttered, clearly taken aback by the question. "It's been a year and a half and we still don't know why they're here. If you'd like to contribute to learning more, you can always enter the science faction. But be warned, they are very selective in the process. It is, after all, the hardest section to get into. They require some schooling."

Holly's too happy demeanor was beginning to grate on my nerves. I just wanted a real shower and a place to sleep.

"Thank you, Holly, could we be shown to our rooms now?" I asked with as much politeness as I could muster.

Holly beamed. "Of course. The safe camp boasts massive underground barracks. We began in small tents in the forest, you know, before moving in here. It's been eight smooth months now and we still have plenty of room for occupants. Tomorrow, please be prepared to choose an occupation and stop by here after breakfast for an official tour."

Harriet and I were roomed together. The room housed a nice bunk bed, two shelves for our clothes and belongings, and a bathroom with a blessed shower. I'd been bathing in cold creeks and river so long now, this commodity seemed like heaven.

"Me first!" cried Harriet and before I could argue her shoes were off and she had the door locked.

I sank onto the bed with a contented sigh. I'd done it; I'd gotten my friends to safety after so long. A harsh knock at the door pulled me out of my thoughts.

"Hello?" I asked as I opened the door. A distinguished older man was there, his military cap sat atop his head and medals pinned to his green military suit spoke volumes. "Yes, how may I help you?"

"Jane Prescott?"

"Yes?" I repeated.

"I am General Styles, head of the combat division in Safe Camp 2. I was wondering if we could chat. Walk with me?"

I glanced at the bathroom door and knew she'd be a while. It was Harriet's first shower in months. Blinking back the fatigue, I complied. "Of course."

"And bring your weapons," he added.

Suddenly suspicious, I looped my belts back on and followed him outside. He said nothing and before long, we came to a guarded room. He entered a code into a panel and the door sprung open.

I gasped upon entering. A day crawler and its twin counterpart lay dead down below a set of stairs. One of their arms was missing, it sat on a table before me.

"Can you identify this Ares?"

Only too well. "I... I killed it, sir."

"With that axe, I presume?"

I was suddenly very confused. How did he know it was my axe? And how did they transport this beast?

"I don't understand..." I was saying before a man in a lab coat came trotting up the steps.

He extended an arm and introduced himself. "Dr. Leston. I understand you killed this day crawler? A very impressive specimen. One of the largest I've seen. May I see your axe?"

I hooked it off my back and handed it to him. "You should know I didn't kill it with this though."

Doctor and general stopped sharply. I held up the proper daggers.

"You have more than one generator?" Doctor Leston's voice was tight with anticipation. "I've only ever seen someone with two generators and still they were just matching pistols." He read the engraved names aloud. "Sage and Thomas."

"Excuse me, but could you explain? What is a generator and why could my axe cut into a day crawler like that?"

The general seemed about to explain before Doctor Leston dove in. An unmistakable excitement edged his voice. "The pulse that knocked out our power, did you feel it?"

I looked between men at a loss but then I remembered what Evan said. "Yes, it was incredibly painful."

"And these weapons, do they hold any sentimental value?"

I nodded. "They were my father's. He bought them in honour of us, his kids. Sage and Thomas were my older siblings. They died in the initial attack, as well as my four other siblings."

Doctor Leston's eyes beamed. "Do you mean to say you have *seven* generators!?" He clasped my hands tightly. "My dear girl, you are incredibly special. This could change the tide of the war in our favour."

I retreated my hands afraid of the responsibility everyone was suddenly trying to push onto me. "Could you please explain?"

Losing his patience, General Styles answered. "That pulse the Ares sent on Earth changed a very select few. We don't know why, but these people gained a sort of... power over weapons with sentimental connection, like you and this axe. It acts as the fuel to the weapon and as far as we know is the only thing capable of piercing night guards and day crawlers."

Doctor Leston continued. "For you to have seven generators is simply mind blowing! Generators are what we call the weapons. The stronger the emotional connection, the stronger the power."

"But I didn't intend for this. I only took them because they were special to me."

Doctor Leston nodded. "We only have three candidates so far with generators and all have similar stories to yours. Sentimental value of the weapon and that the pulse was a painful experience. We keep close contact with the bases in Europe and Australia and they too have seen people with similar abilities. But none have chopped an arm clean off like this."

"Are you saying this axe is more powerful?"

"Perhaps. Also," he pulled out a clipboard and pen and began writing notes. "How did you remove the poison from the daggers?"

"I didn't. It just slipped off. Almost like the dagger itself repelled the poison. When I picked it up, it was completely dry, it didn't even stink."

Doctor Leston furiously wrote and wished to examine each of my blades for possible specializing.

"Also, how did you guys even find me? I just got here."

"We screen the weapons brought into the base. I knew the cut had to be made by a blade and yours was too perfect not to be it," the general replied then turned to Doctor Leston. "Well, there you have it, doctor. Miss Prescott, would you consider joining the combat faction under an elite team? I am hoping to send out the soldiers with generators on special missions. The training would be extensive but you'd be making a real difference."

"What kind of missions?" I asked tentatively.

"You'd get to kill as many day crawlers and night guards as you want."

I didn't even have to think. "I'm in."

CHAPTER FIVE

The air was still and not a bird or bug could be heard within the city limits. Sweat trickled down my forehead in the heat. It was past midday now. I gripped my axe harder and discreetly peered over the side of the three-story building. If a day crawler could be bored, this one was. It almost looked like it was picking at its nails. Still, a day crawler was dangerous and every precaution was necessary. I scanned the rooftops for my three comrades in arms. Cedar crouched on the building across from me, a massive rifle in her hands. On the street below, I knew Max and Keith were ready on either side of the Ares. Both guys elected that Cedar and I find the twin but this one was proving to be difficult. They never strayed too far from each other and given that the lazy one down below was so relaxed, it stood to reason that the other one was in a similar state. But no matter how many rooftops we'd scanned, the beast was nowhere to be seen. I was almost ready to let this lazy bone have it when the building beneath me shook nearly knocking me off my feet. Something had slammed into it. When I turned around, I was face to dace with a ferocious day crawler. Saliva dripped from its mouth and it exhaled a deep guttural growl. The building beneath our feet became unstable under the weight of the creature. The doorway leading out was blocked. I was trapped. If Keith didn't act soon, I'd be done for.

A glowing blue shot zoomed past me and nicked its arm. Cedar was a terrible shot but the wound was still sizeable. The Ares got angry and swung at me with its massive arm. I barely ducked out of the way in time. Down below, I could hear Max shooting his pistol and Cedar her rifle. Keith wold be spearing it in the eyes right about now, so all I had to do was bide my time. I lunged and swung my axe with ease. After a year of practice, my skills had become infinitely better. The day crawler batted at me despite the gash in its torso. The roof cracked under the shift in weight and I dropped to my knees. The day crawler slammed his fist and I barely rolled out of its reach in time. I could hear my heart pounding in my ears. Shaken from the near miss I scrambled to my feet, taking a fighting stance.

"Anytime now, Keith," I muttered, barely dodging another swing. The roof didn't have much time left. Impatient, I jumped up and swung as hard as I could with both hands. A golden arc of light swept forth slicing the Ares's head off with a sickening shloop. Head and body tumbled and crashed over the side of the building. Glass and debris went flying. The ground shook upon impact quickly followed by its counterpart.

I stood peering over the edge. "What gives?" I shouted and saw Keith stumble to retrieve his spear.

After cleanup, we rendezvoused at the truck and zoomed away.

"You aren't mad, are you?" asked Cedar tentatively.

I turned to her in the back seat. "Of course not! Although your aim could use some practice. You nearly shot me in the back."

Cedar apologized again while Keith said nothing. I knew he was his hardest critic, so I also said nothing. Max, however, was seething at the gash on his arm.

"Any closer and it would have disemboweled me!" he glared at Keith through the rear-view.

"Give it a rest, they are still learning."

This was only our third couple in training now. It was tough work and dangerous, but Max and I made a good team, when he wasn't busy losing his temper.

When we arrived back at camp, the sun was setting and a chill seized the air.

"I'll go log in the crawler's location. You go eat," ordered Max.

He was in his late thirties and treated me like a little sister. I loved him for it, especially when it meant I could find Harry and the others sooner. We'd made a pact on day one to eat together every night and we more or less kept it.

Harry gave me a big hug when she saw me. "Did you get it? I always get so nervous. When Cindy told me you guys were going out today, I dropped a whole tray of dishes."

She proceeded to tell me every mundane detail about her day. Somehow, I loved it. It was like a shred of normalcy among the horrible reality we were now living. A romantic dream of what life used to be: simple and carefree, although we didn't know it. Our biggest worry used to be money, money, money and now it was just plain survival.

Luke plopped down at the table. He and Karl had joined combat while Evan and Samuel were on the maintenance crew. Harriet was in kitchen, of course.

"You would not believe the day we had! Karl and I were set to patrol the area and of course we got lost…"

I zoned him out as I did most nights. He liked to complain too much. Funny, I'd never noticed it when we were dating. I saw Max head to the table where Cindy, Harriet's workmate, sat. Word was the two had a thing going. It must be nice to meet someone. A little ray of sunshine in this hellhole, but who had the time?

Thinking of Max turned my thoughts more sombre. More and more day crawlers and night guards were seen in town next to the woods. What did it mean? Every time we seemed to get a step ahead in this war, the Ares seemed to repopulate. Would there be no end? Would they keep coming forever?

A tap on my shoulder brought me back to the table.

"Jane, can I talk to you for a second? In private?"

Refraining from rolling my eyes proved difficult. There was only one reason Luke used my full name.

It had been almost six months since Luke had asked me out and to be honest it was getting rather tiring. This time I'd thought for sure he'd moved on.

"Yes, Luke, what is it?" I asked.

He rocked back and forth on his heels, feigning nervousness. "I was wondering if you'd like to take a stroll with me around campus tomorrow… Just us?"

"No." I responded too quickly and he frowned.

Grabbing my arm, he pulled me further into our 'private' little alcove. "Why not? It'll be fun. Don't you ever want to give us a shot together again? We were great, *are* great."

I rubbed my temples. "No." I said it firmly and with a tone that brooked no argument.

But this was Luke. "Look, Jay. I know you want me. Why else have you stayed single so long? You don't need to keep playing hard to get. I'm already interested."

The hallway suddenly felt stuffy with his ego inflating as it was. "Look, Luke. I don't want to date you because you complain all the time, you're irresponsible, and when it mattered most, you showed an incredible lack of character. I have forgiven you for it, there is honestly no hard feelings there, but that doesn't mean we need to date. I haven't seen you act in any way that would make me believe you are a different person."

Giving him space to lick his wounds, I turned on my heel and returned to the table, where Harriet had a pained expression but Evan, Karl, and Samuel had bets going.

"Seriously! I can't believe he asked again!" cried Karl as he handed the currency, chocolate, to Evan and Samuel. "I'm even his best friend too!"

I laughed although even I had to admit his persistence was impressive.

Just then, warning lights flashed red through every corridor and dorm room; it was an emergency. I hadn't even had time to put my gear away so I slung it over my shoulder. A voice over the intercom gave instructions for all non-combat personnel to follow safety procedures. Karl, Luke, and I ran to our posts as fast as we could.

"Would Jane Prescott please check in to the Red Room? Jane Prescott?"

I blew a kiss to Karl and Luke asking them to be safe as I ran to the Red Room - a conference room specifically used for highly classified meetings.

Max, Cedar, and Keith were already geared up and seated by the time I took my seat. General Styles was running the briefing.

"A night guard is prowling our camp as we speak. It is trying to get in but has been unsuccessful so far. We think it is slightly confused by the thick metal and that we are so far underground. But these creatures are smart and learn quickly. Keith and Cedar, you will cover Max and Jane's old post. Jane and Max, it's up to you to kill it. This is a confidential mission, do not fail."

"At least transporting the alien will be easy," joked Keith.

"How did it find us? And so far in the forest?"

General Styles clearly expected my question and didn't batt an eye. "I will debrief you once you return. Dismissed."

It was already nerve-wracking enough to find an Ares so deep in the woods but it was worse that our commanding officers wouldn't tell us anything.

"Maybe it was by accident?"

I gave Max a look, knowing full well he didn't believe that either. He said nothing.

Slipping outside the base and securing the door was the easy part; it became difficult trying to sneak up on the night guard. Night guards had an intense sense of smell and their ability to read body temperature made it difficult to hide. As always when I faced theses beasts my heart picked up its pace and my palms became sweaty. The best way to attack was head on; only then could you catch it by surprise--maybe. After a quick moment of silent gesturing, Max went left and I went right. My axe was raised. I was ready to strike.

Slowly, I creeped forward, careful to stay silent. I held my breath but just as I was within range the Ares sensed me and whipped its tail around, knocking me to the ground. Struggling to catch my breath I wondered, just for a second, if I had broken something. Aware of the night guard about to pounce on me I shook it off, desperately patting the ground for my axe; but it was nowhere in sight. My head was spinning, but I had to move. The night guard was nearly on me when the pop of Max's pistol rang through the air. I felt intense relief which suddenly, miraculously, cleared my head. Enraged, the alien swung about and charged Max. But he was out of bullets. As he tried to reload, he dropped them all on the ground. Eyes wide, he ran, leading the beast away from the camp giving me time to gain my bearings.

"Forget the axe!" I growled, Max needed me. I slipped out Gideon and Thomas and flung them after the creature. The moment they left my hands, a blue light emanated from behind and they shot forth at an incredible speed, following the alien around every twist and bend. I found my legs and began running after them. "Come on, come on." I muttered. As I pressed on so did the knives until they found their mark and pierced his chest. I skidded to a stop, balancing on the balls of my feet, ready to jump out of the way should the night guard still have it in him to attack me. A bang permeated the air. I guessed Max was able to get one bullet in the chamber of his gun after all which pierced a gaping hole to the head of the monstrous Ares. He dropped dead in a thunderous shower of branches.

I checked to make sure I was okay. Nothing a few Band-aids and a hot shower couldn't fix. Max helped me stand before heading back inside. Everyone was still on high alert. It stood to reason that if one Ares had made its way into our camp, more would be coming.

CHAPTER SIX

We'd been waiting in the Red Room for nearly two hours before General Styles came in, followed by Doctor Leston. Cedar and Keith were still in training but were permitted into the meeting anyway, given the situation.

The general took off his cap and gave a weary sigh. "It's worse than we thought." After a heavy pause he continued. "The man safe camp in Mexico has fallen. As we speak, hundreds of refugees are on their way here. We have some room but not much. All of you will have two or three more people in your rooms, including everyone else stationed at this base."

The weight of his words pressed down upon all of us.

"You all have permission to speak freely."

"What about the other generators? Where are they?" blurted out Cedar.

"We have no idea who has survived. We can't even project numbers. All we know is communication is lost. The last thing we heard was a Code Black and then that night guard was spotted outside our door."

We all knew a Code Black meant little to no hope. Hundreds of refugees might have been an overstatement.

"What's the plan then? Will they come for us next?" asked Max.

The general nodded. "We have to assume so. We are staying on high alert. Leadership is considering disbanding the base. It might be safer in tiny groups, as we'd be harder to track. They wanted all of your opinions."

"No." I said. "We cannot send these people out there on their own. More than half have no idea how to defend themselves against wild animals, much less against the Ares. And how would they provide food and shelter for themselves? No. We have to find another way."

General Styles folded his arms. "I agree. But the initial reports said they attacked in a horde and we only have you four warriors to defend this place."

Doctor Leston finally spoke. "These creatures are abandoning every behavioural trait we've ever learned. They attacked together in the middle of the untamed jungles of Mexico. We couldn't even get trucks through there. They worked together, which they never do. What little communication we had with France was severed a month back, and the last thing they said was the same: they were attacked exactly as the Mexico base. Night guards showed up in the day and days crawlers at night. I believe this is the Ares' final assault; this is it for humanity."

Max scoffed angrily. "Then how do we come out alive? Most of Earth's population is gone. We can't sit here and defend ourselves, we'd be sitting ducks. And we can't do a frontal attack because only *our* weapons can take out the big guys." He turned to me with a pleading look in his eyes and a knot of dread twisted in my stomach. "Jane. I think our best option is to leave. It's our only option.

Humanity's only option." He took my arms in his hands. "It's been over two years and we still don't even know why or how the Ares got here. Maybe they're here just to kill us. For sport?"

I wanted to vomit. It was almost logical and that was sickening. But I could tell he was right. The heat of the base and all the humans grouped together like this was easy tracking for the night guards. I turned to the general. "I think Max is right."

The general nodded solemnly. "I have to debrief the other sectors. Everyone should start packing up now and be prepared to leave in the morning."

I hugged Max a long time, hoping one day to see him again. I'd be leaving with Evan, Luke, Karl, Samuel, and Harriet. A group bigger than that was asking for attention and he had his own loved ones to look after.

"Be safe," Max whispered in my ear.

He kissed my forehead before turning to leave. My eyes glistened with unshed tears and I ran toward the kitchen hoping my friends might be grouped there. I found Luke almost immediately, but he looked upset.

"Who was that?" He pointed after Max and there was an accusatory edge sharpening his tone. Rolling my eyes, I grasped his arm and continued walking toward the main sitting area. "Max. My co-worker. Come on, we're leaving. Do you know where Karl is?" I filled him in and he said he knew where the guys were. He went to get them, while I started looking for Harriet. I found her in our dorm crying. When I opened the door, she gave me a massive bear hug.

"Thank goodness, you're okay! I was worried sick! Where were you!?" Fresh tears, but this time, joyful ones, streamed down her cheeks. I patted her shoulder and quickly informed her of the situation.

Pale faced, she sunk down on the bed in a daze. "I…I don't know if I can make it out there again."

I sat beside her. "Yes, you can! Don't say that! All of us are going to be together. Right now, the guys are gathering their stuff; we should, too."

I moved to gather our things but she remained still. Slowly, I sat back down.

Tears threatened to fall and her voice broke. "No, Jane. I mean I'm pregnant. Karl is the father." She started sobbing and I felt my heart ready to rip apart and hugged her fiercely.

"You know what, Harry, we're going to make it. We'll get supplies at hospitals and… And we could somehow get an ultra sound machine to work. We can do this. Besides, if we stay, we definitely won't make it."

She opened and closed her hands. "I don't know…it seems like a stretch." Doubt edged her voice.

I moved to crouch down below her to better see her face. "Harriet. Listen to me. If we do not leave, we *will* die. And your baby."

She refused to meet my eyes. "You don't *know* that."

"Fine." I flung myself down on the bed again. "I'll stay here with you. We'll make a life here."

Confusion and fear passed through her eyes. "You can't do that!"

I shrugged. "Why not? If you can, I definitely can."

Harriet faced me and was nearly shouting. "But you'll be in danger."

I sat up. "No less than you three. You know Karl would never leave you."

At the mention of his name she looked down. "Actually, now that you say it, I think he won't let me stay." I could see the gears turning in her thoughts.

"I promise Harry, we'll protect your kid."

An inner strength I always knew she possessed hardened her eyes and she gave me a curt nod. "Yes. I'll get packing."

Efficiently both of us packed one duffel bag each of things we'd need: water bottles, toiletries, underwear, and so on. Travelling north seemed the safest option, as the Ares weren't particularly fond of colder climates. A part of me wondered if places like northern Canada and Russia were even aware of the alien invasion.

"Nonsense," I muttered to myself as I zipped my bag shut. "Ready?" I asked Harriet.

Harriet stood and sighed. "Yes. Where are we meeting the guys?"

"The cafeteria, where we usually sit."

Harriet sighed again and took a step back to take in our little dorm. Samuel's drawings hung on the walls, making the room feel homier. Somehow, Harriet had managed to get her hands on some old clothes to make throw pillows out of. Luke welded us some metal art that hung in the bathroom. All these mementos made our room like a little home and now we were uprooted… again.

CHAPTER SEVEN

We reached the cafeteria and unsurprisingly, the guys were all packed and ready before us. A sense of urgency filled the air. Everyone walked with purpose and shared that same hard worried expression. Every moment this place became more and more unsafe, what with the Ares getting closer and closer. The roof above us and ground below began to rumble and I could hear what could only be the angry roars of the Ares in the distance.

"Samuel! Lead as many people as you can to the access port in repair room five!" He nodded knowing the escape hatch I meant. Quickly, I hugged everyone in the group before practically shoving them in the right direction.

Luke lingered. "Wait, what about you?"

Max, Cedar, and Keith ran up. I nodded to them. "Go, Luke. I'll meet up with you later."

I couldn't tell if he believed me but he ran to catch up after the others. The four of us rushed to the main hangar doors waiting with anticipation, weapons poised. A loud banging came from the other side with scratching noises, much like when a dog scratches begging to come inside.

Suddenly, all sound ceased. Everything was eerily quiet. An odd scent permeated the air.

Cedar lowered her gun. "Are they gone?" She sounded doubtful.

"Ready your weapons!" Max looked near panicked. I'd never seen him like this. He was shaking and pale and sweat trickled down his brow.

"What's wrong?" I asked dreading the answer.

"When I lived in New York... This smell..."

I grabbed him. "Max! Keep it together or I'll-"

Metal scraping against metal cut me off. I whipped around in time to see a giant hook penetrate the hangar doors. That weird smell intensified. The hook turned prying back the metal like butter. The hook disappeared and its owner passed through.

All of us were taken aback. A human-like figure stood above us at about eight feet tall. His skin was grey and he had four arms, two of which held sharp massive hooks firmly. His eyes were yellow and he had a sadistic grin plastered on his face. He held up one of his empty fists and hundreds of two-horns came bursting in. The four of us reacted as one and began shooting and swinging but they paid us no mind. Even if we injured or killed them. Snarling, they rushed past us. Ready to kill. My heart rate increased. Dread of the worst kind clutched my body in a furious grip. There was no way we'd get them all.

"Look out front!" yelled Keith, focusing his aim toward the doors.

Day crawlers and night guards rumbled in, their speed and ferocity had accelerated to heights even I'd never seen. I swung my axe as hard as I could taking down monster after monster, but more and more poured through the now sizeable door. The grey alien from before was nowhere to be seen. My eyes darted about the room but I couldn't see past the swarm of Ares. Samuel had mentioned once a fourth kind of Ares, but no one paid him mind. He'd heard it from a stranger who'd heard it from a friend of a friend who'd heard it from a dying man. Stories like that just weren't reliable and yet here we were, witnessing the terrifying truth: Ares were far more intelligent than we gave them credit for.

They just kept coming and coming, swarming about us. Screams echoed down the halls as Ares' mowed down any person they found. Blood and sweat filled my senses but I kept swinging and throwing. Relentlessly mowing down the aliens. Blue and yellow arcs of light flashed brightly in the night but it wasn't enough. They just kept coming. One went down and was quickly replaced by five more. I swallowed the urge to vomit. My arms felt weak but I couldn't stop. I had to push on. I and the others were all that stood between them and the humans.

"I'm out! I'm out of-" Cedar's ear-splitting scream was cut off by the sickening crack of her spine. The noises that followed were too gruesome to focus on. Fuelled by anger at the loss of my friend, I swung harder.

Max's bullets had long since stopped spraying. He died with dignity. Or at least that's what I told myself, because I couldn't watch. Keith swung his spear frantically, but a night crawler whipped its tail, knocking him to the ground. His spear sprang from his hand. I threw my last dagger, Lynn, at it and the beast fell down. Hauling him to his feet and retrieving his spear, Keith stabbed the beast to make sure it was truly dead. We went back to back swinging and thrusting. Golden arcs of light swept from our weapons and across the army of Ares. Would the cry of innocents never cease? Or the swarm of monsters?

A massive day crawler crouched through the door, I swung my axe in an attempt to behead the beast but missed and a part of the ceiling fell on its foot. Enraged, it swatted me and I fell backward, knocking into Keith. He lost his footing. A two-horn stabbed him lifeless. Helplessly I watched his body being dragged into the throng to be mutilated.

Hot angry tears dripped down my cheeks. How could this be happening? I picked myself up and madly swung my weapon back and forth. Blindingly bright arcs swept forth, larger than I'd ever made before, killing any Ares near me. But I hardly noticed. The only thought on my mind was to kill.

I don't know how long I went off for before dropping to my knees in defeat. If generators couldn't survive the attack, what were the odds my friends made it out? What was the point? The clang of my axe on the concrete cut into the silence.

Looking up, I finally noticed two-horns had me completely surrounded. Day crawlers and night guards hung back and a slow clapping sounded from above.

The grey alien returned with that same aggravating grin. "That truly was delightful," he said... in English? "So. Congratulations! You've won!"

Huh?

CHAPTER EIGHT

"You've won," he repeated less enthusiastically. It seemed he didn't like to repeat himself.

I was completely and utterly confused. Managing to get my feet under me, I stood up. Now I felt less like a grasshopper to be squished.

I aimed my axe at him. "What do you mean? Explain!" I demanded.

He smirked. "You'll see, puny human. Gather the daggers she lost!" he ordered, and all the day crawlers lumbered around searching for my family of weapons.

Uncorking a glass vile, the grey alien threw it at my feet. The strange smell from before intensified and almost immediately my sense grew fuzzy. I lost my grip on my axe and my vision went blurry. Without realizing it, I slumped to my knees and my eyes were heavy. Try as I might, I just... couldn't... stay... awake...

I woke slowly on a dusty stone floor chained to the wall, my belongings nowhere in sight. The first thing I noticed was my sore back followed quickly by my parched throat and the remnants of a nightmare I couldn't remember. It was no matter; the dream was always the same.

Shivering, I slowly sat up. The room was dark and even after my eyes adjusted, all I could make out was the outline of a door and the straw that served as a bed. The room was very small and as I reached out to touch the walls, my hand met with cool stone. Where was I? I didn't bother calling out but lay back down, trying to sleep. My eyelids drooped and sleep swiftly overtook me.

I'd been awake for several boring hours before the door slid open silently. The light was blindingly bright and five oddly dressed Ares entered. I could only assume they were women. They had four arms like the grey warrior but were only about six feet tall with grey skin and gross, long black ponytails. Their dresses were identical and very plain.

Lifeless yellow eyes greeted me. They curtsied in unison and the first one, the one with the keys, unchained me. "This way please," she said, motioning towards the hall.

"Where are we going? Where is my stuff?"

She smiled but it didn't reach her eyes. "Your things will be returned to you tomorrow morning. But first, you must wash up for the banquet. Please, follow us."

I stepped out of the cell. Any thoughts of escape were out of the question without my gear, not to mention the guards that were stationed everywhere.

Bright torches lined the walls of the corridor as well as many doors. Doors like mine. Just how many prisoners were there?

"How many humans have you captured?" I asked, forcing calm to my voice.

"Oh, you are mistaken. You are the only human we've obtained."

I walked along silently until we came to a corridor of columns and open air. My first instinct was to jump but halted when I realized we were floating along in cold, dark space, with Earth shrinking in the distance. I reached my hand through the columns and touched cold glass, so clear it was invisible.

"What is this place?"

"Welcome to Trireme, the home planet of the Ares."

"Planet?" I sputtered.

Urging me forward, we continued walking.

"Oh yes." Finally, a speck of emotion lit her eyes. "Our planet is like a magnificent ship floating through space. Incredible, is it not?"

Well I couldn't disagree, but I wouldn't give her the satisfaction and so remained silent. It was strange; this place was obviously far superior in technology than Earth, but everything was made of stone and dust collected on the floors. Perhaps that was only because we were obviously in the dungeons. She sniffed and opened a large wooden door.

You'd think shoving me inside was rude enough, but then they stripped me of my clothes and practically drowned me in large hot pools. Steam ascended from the waters and orange flowers were scattered everywhere. I couldn't decipher the scent but soon, I was drenched in it.

It wasn't long before I was scrubbed clean and ushered into what could only be described as a beauty salon. I was propped on a single stool. One girl began doing my hair, the other focused on perfumes and cosmetics. The other three brought clothing forward and assessed my size. However, only one spoke to me, the same girl as before.

"You are so tiny!"

"I'll have you know, I am a girl of average height on Earth…." Why was I arguing? What did it matter?

"Please, put this on. His Highness has made it specially to represent planet Earth."

Surveying the rich fabric, I held up the dress which lead me to assume that the king was crazy or cruel. Suddenly, I felt like picking the perfect outfit was the most important thing and this heap of outrageous rags was unfit. My hands found my hips.

"Listen, lady. This dress is ridiculous. The cultures of my planet are very different. We have hundreds of languages, no one shares the same traditional dress, we even eat different food! I am supposed to represent my home planet tonight and it's kind of important seeing as I'm the only human on board! So, shove it and let me pick something else out!"

The reaction I got was gasps of horror and a look of utter contempt.

"This isn't a choice. King Memign had this made specially for you!" She shoved the dress my way.

Expressionless, they stood there patiently waiting for me to take the clothes. Finally, I came to the realization I could never overpower five tall broad ladies unarmed and I surrendered. Slipping the dress over my head and dipping my feet into some boots, I placidly let them add jewelry and ornaments to my neck, arms, and hair.

When they finally stepped back to allow me a peek, I couldn't help but giggle. I looked ridiculous! Their proud expression faded to confused frowns. Their high and mighty king thought *this* would represent Earth? The dress was a turtle-neck with all sorts of colours floating down my bust in chaotic disarray. The colourful shoots also grew off my arms. All I could think of were those awful fringe coats from the seventies.

It was slim fitted around my hips but shot straight out like a tutu at my knees. I could barely walk. The boots were too high and were a strange shiny black fabric with a diamond etched print. None of the colours matched. To top it off, they'd painted my face in every colour imaginable. I looked like a gay pride float. This was how I was representing my home? The giggles subsided and I felt only anger now and my hands turned to fists.

"You people killed billions of innocent people and *this* is how you choose to display us!? It's downright insulting!"

I grabbed the nearest vase and threw it at one of the quintuplets. Screaming, they scattered. The one bearing the keys remained the only calm one. A stern, parent-like expression decorated her face. Grabbing my arm, she dragged me back outside. We came to a set of doors and I could only assume the banquet lay beyond.

"Tomorrow you may pick whatever outfit you desire but tonight you must wear this." She spoke through gritted teeth. "You are fortunate enough to have this gown. Made by the king. The *king*. Refuse, and you shall attend naked." And with that she propelled me through the enormous wooden doors.

CHAPTER NINE

Immediately, I felt all eyes on me. Two guards, who were apparently waiting for me, escorted me to my seat. I sat among beings who were obviously not Ares. One had two heads, another mottled green skin and scales. I counted sixteen of us, and we all wore ridiculous outfits that were utterly horrible.

Food was served and we were forced to sit and watch the Ares dance and make merry. The room the party was hosted in had large wooden chandeliers covered in dripping candles, and floor-to-ceiling drapes festooned the walls. Even from where I was sitting, I could tell the fabric was rich and that in here, the floors and pillars were of polished stone similar to marble, but seeing as this wasn't Earth, not likely the same. Course after course was served and although the food looked inedible, I forced myself to try it, keeping in mind I would need my strength. Luckily, some of it wasn't all that bad.

As the night waned, King Memign stood from his gold gilded throne to make a speech. "My honoured subjects! Thank you for attending this twenty-first annual First Feast!" Applauding rippled throughout the room. The king continued even though his words were slurred and he swayed on the spot. "Tomorrow's," he hiccuped, "tournament promises to be our greatest yet! We conquered many prominent civilizations. The great Ewer!" A roar of excitement rumbled through the room and the man beside me clenched his fist.

"Was that your planet?" I spoke before thinking but didn't regret the question. Slowly, he turned to me and nodded. His skin was incredible, it looked like glass. Would a bad fall cause him to shatter? I focused my attention back to what he was saying. "They sent a burst of energy which destroyed our power sources then they slaughtered my wife and child in front of me. When most of our population was gone, they took me."

Exactly like Earth! "That burst of energy, was it painful?"

"Yes. But my family said they hadn't felt a thing."

Suddenly, an odd thought hit me. "You speak English?"

The glass man's chuckle was drowned out by the roaring of drunk guests. The king easily riled them up naming all the planets they'd conquered, Earth among them.

"No. When they took you, they drugged you and implanted a chip in your head. It affects the part of your body that processes language. Although some Ares are more learned than others. To me, you are speaking Ewerian."

"Hm. Convenient." I thought of the first grey warrior I'd met, he spoke English. Were the Ares too lazy? I gazed at all the men on the table around me. Earth alone had hundreds of languages, not to mention everyone here at the table. And this was the twenty-first games which meant dozens more planets. On second thought, a language chip was brilliant!

The Ewerian cut into my thoughts. "What happened to your home?"

"The same." I didn't want to get into details. "I was picked up just yesterday. How long have you been here?"

"About a week. My planet was easy prey for the low-ranking Ares to destroy as we live in an entirely crystalized environment." He paused and a sadness passed through his eyes. "Lived."

I touched his shoulder sympathetically. "My family was killed in front of me as well." I stretched forth my hand. "My name is-"

He put his fingers to my lips, stopping me. "Don't. It will make tomorrow harder."

With the other hand he took mine and squeezed it gently. In companionable silence we ate. It felt good to make somewhat of a friend. The honoured guests continued screaming and clapping as King Memign listed all the conquered planets and went into detail about their faults. Everyone at our table became more and more aggravated but could do nothing. Each of us had two guards watching our every move and we had no weapons. Then there was the matter of being on Trireme. I had no way of returning home. It was all very frustrating and scary.

At the end of the exhausting banquet, I was led back to my solitary cell by the same five ladies. "Why am I here?"

The lady with the key unlocked the door and turned to me. "You will fight in our great annual tournament."

Swallowing my shock and horror I managed to ask: "If I refuse?"

She folded her hands decorously in front of her robes. "This is a great honour for you. The Ares live for this tournament." Misjudging my expression, she patted my hand and I resisted the urge to recoil in disgust. "Fret not, tomorrow everything shall be explained."

I lay on my pitiful pile of straw and stared into the inky blackness. I would be fighting to the death tomorrow. Perhaps this was okay. Earth was a destroyed dust pile and all my friends were undoubtedly gone so I really had nothing left. Still, I forced my eyes shut trying to sleep. I'd need my strength if I wanted to win. I guess in the end, despite my rationalizing, I knew in the deep recesses of my soul, I wanted to live.

I awoke to someone shaking my shoulder and opened my eyes with a start.

"Jane." A voice fiercely whispered.

"Mom?" I whispered back.

"Janey, you need to leave. This is a dangerous place. Leave now while you can!" Her voice grew urgent. I reached out into the inky blackness to reach her but she was just beyond my grasp.

"Mom, where are you? How did you find me?"

Her voice cracked as she spoke. "Jane. I love you. I love you…." She was fading and a familiar scene became apparent. When I opened my cell door I was in my kitchen once more. I shut my eyes to the horror and tears violently rushed down my cheeks. Backing into my cell I shut the door firmly but when I turned around the room had morphed into the kitchen. Even clenching my eyes shut couldn't block out the scene.

No matter what I faced tomorrow, it could never be as bad as that Christmas day.

I awoke panting for breath and sat up quickly, trying to brush away what haunted me. So much for keeping up my strength for the awaiting day. Yearning for the light, I didn't sleep for the rest of the night.

CHAPTER TEN

I could hear the thundering roars of the masses far above me and, beyond the iron gate, a large stonework arena stretched forth. Sand bathed the ground and I was instantly reminded of a gladiatorial ring. My stomach clenched.

Just moments earlier, King Memign had held a small ceremony in honour of us fighters. It was unnerving what I'd learned.

"Ladies and gentlemen, welcome to Trireme. Today you shall die in the most honourable way – in glorious battle! Four battles with four fighters, the winners shall then fight in a final fifth battle. The winner is granted the honour to become my royal concubine." He winked at a bald purple skinned alien with three eyes and tentacles whose gender I could not even begin to discern. Clearing his throat, the arrogant king continued, his tone drenched with mock disappointment. "I've been hearing that some of you don't like the idea of fighting in this tournament." His face turned cold. "But I'll have you know, I gave you your newfound powers and I can take them away just as easily." Purposely he stared hard at each and every one of us. Gasps and murmurs rippled through the room, including my own. What did he mean he gave us our powers? A thought bloomed in my mind. Every one of these prisoners all had similar stories to mine, a painful pulse of energy coupled with losing loved ones in some tragic way that was connected with the Ares. I knew the king was telling the truth.

Obviously satisfied with our alarmed responses the king resumed his happy demeanor. "Refusal to fight results in death and anyone who dares think of rebelling shall meet a fate worse than death. I shall meet you in the arena!" His ornate gold encrusted robes swooshed behind him as he left us and everyone stood in silent defeat. What fate could be worse than becoming his concubine? I shuddered. The king stood three feet above me easily and constantly reeked of piss and alcohol. I had to escape!

We were separated and our weapons were returned to us before being forced up a long dark corridor. At the end was a locked iron gate.

Suddenly, the cries of the crowd subsided and a hush fell over the arena as four iron doors slowly slid open, including my own.

The guards posted to watch me pointed their hooks in my face, forcing me to step into the arena.

A deafening noise of excitement boomed through the arena. Thousands of onlookers cheered and waved their arms frantically, waiting with painful anticipation to see us die. Surveying my opponents – the purple alien, the two-headed alien, and a little pink man who constantly hovered above the ground – made me feel sick. I felt relief that I wasn't facing the glass man. My palms were sweaty and my heart raced in anticipation of the ensuing battle but

I was able to stay calm. Our faces were devoid of emotion but the two-headed alien whipped out his gun and fired at the purple woman. I didn't have time to see the outcome as the little pink one came at me, a small dagger in hand. Choosing Thomas and Ryan seemed a smart choice, as they were my biggest blades. The hovering man looked shocked at how many weapons I carried. I purposely left me axe sheathed; perhaps I wouldn't have to kill him in the end. He was, after all, as innocent as I. He slashed at me and I dodged. The blades in my hand heated up but still I refused to lash out. I kicked the man and he fell backward, hard. Regret and shame clenched my stomach until it was almost painful. An apology was right on my lips when he growled and flew at me.

We were locked in a knife fight, him thrusting and me eluding.

"We don't have to fight!" I said, trying to negotiate.

"The king said fight or die!" He lunged again and barely missed my neck.

Biting back anger I tried again. "He is just trying to scare us. If we fight together, we may have a chance!"

He nicked my arm and I couldn't resist the urge to retaliate. I threw Ryan and the familiar blue light shot forth, propelling the blade into his thigh. Slowly the pink man ceased hovering and gently planted both feet on the ground. Purply liquid seeped out of the wound. Real anger burned in his eyes and he sprang forth more ferociously, despite the wound. Reacting just as quickly, I dodged his thrust and turned abruptly, throwing Lynn into the mix. The dagger pierced his shoulder. My hands began to hurt from gripping the daggers so tightly.

The anger inside me faded. Yes, the man was attacking me, but still, why should we bow to the Ares' whims?

"Please, I don't want to hurt you!" I pleaded again, putting my hands up in a gesture of amity.

He seemed to be growing faint and knelt on the ground to catch his breath. Tentatively, hoping to convey peace, I came close. "I'm begging you, please. Don't fight me, fight *with* me."

I didn't see the blade coming but he missed, slashing my arm instead of the intended lethal blow. Instinctively, I embedded Thomas straight into his chest. Shock lit up both our faces only his went blank as he tumbled to the ground.

Obstreperous cries rose from the audience but I could barely hear it as I stared at the bloody dagger still clenched in my hands.

A bullet whizzed past my face bringing me back, its blue light unmistakable. I didn't have time to process what I'd just done as the two-headed alien shot at me. I did a tuck-and-roll, getting out of the way just in time. Glancing toward the other end of the arena, I could see the purple woman face-down on the ground. I supposed she lost their tête-à-tête. Again, time to process was lost as I flung Tyler and Sage at his weapon and wrist, hoping to dislodge it from his arms. But the alien was quick on his feet and jumped out of the way, shooting as he went. Gideon was my last dagger and again I tried to remove the gun, but a bullet knocked it off its trajectory. Planting my feet, I slowly, I unsheathed my axe. I truly didn't want to hurt him but he was making it more and more difficult.

The sand made running and dodging difficult but I was catching on.

Quite suddenly I decided this alien would be the one to win. I threw my axe to the ground and held up my hands in surrender. Thunderous outrage boomed through the arena. I'd killed enough innocent people today and I already felt horrible, so it was nice to be going on my own terms. The two-headed alien hesitated for a moment but reconsidering, raised his gun and aimed. A sword split through his chest. He hung there suspended upright as lethal amounts of blood spilled onto the sandy ground.

The purple alien came around and without hesitation grabbed me round the neck with one of her tentacles and began squeezing. She lifted me into the air and I scratched and clawed gasping for breath. Adrenaline burned behind her eyes but she didn't have much time left. Three large gaping holes spilled her blood across her body. My legs flailed. Just as I began seeing white dots and my head throbbed violently her grip loosened and the alien slumped to the ground. I coughed and inhaled heavily, grateful not to have murdered anyone else.

The crowd's half-hearted cheers were silenced by the king.

"The human wins! Crown the victor!"

A troupe of armed guards rushed to comply with the king's orders. A purple-leafed crown was placed on my head and my weapons were taken from me immediately. They heaved the corpses into wheelbarrows and carried them away, I didn't want to imagine where.

I was led through a wooden door where the five same ladies awaited.

"Bandage her up and make sure she gets well rested for tonight's banquet," one of the guards said and then we were alone.

They stitched up my wound and wrapped it tightly. The day was filled with pampering and bathing. It seemed I was never clean enough. Almost like they thought my pink skin was filthy and it should be paler, like their own deathly pallor.

Eventually, I was led to a dimly lit room with a large luscious bed. Curtains swayed in the breeze. When I peered through the window, the sheer drop was at least fifty feet and men guarded the bottom.

"There will be a man at the door if you need anything. We will be here in a few hours to prepare you for the evening's festivities."

Each lady exited and all was quiet. Distantly I could hear the cries from the arena. The next battle had obviously begun. Tomorrow would have to be different. Perhaps at the party tonight I could convince the others to form a coup.

Choosing not to overexert myself, I crawled onto the bed and slept hard.

The girls had to rouse me from my nightmare for which I was all too grateful. The dress they prepared for me this evening was no better than the last. Pink rosettes covered my bust and at the back, an unmanageable red bow reared its ugly head. The dress offered no shape which made it comfortable, but the shade of pink washed me out and the brown, thigh-high boots were covered in what looked like dog hair.

"Is this also meant to represent earth?" I asked sarcastically.

The only lady who spoke squinted her eyes, as if begging me to talk back any further. A part of me almost preferred going naked to wearing this atrocity.

The banquet was held in a different hall than the night before but was no less extravagant. We were still forced to sit amongst ourselves and listen to the king's narcissistic ramblings but much to my relief, the glass man greeted me with a smile, equally as happy to see that I was alive.

"Let us enjoy this night together," he quietly said.

Knowing what he meant, I agreed. In length he told me of his home and family and I listened intently, drinking in all the knowledge of another planet I'd never imagined truly existed. In kind I returned the favour, he seemed particularly interested in grass and trees.

"Tomorrow we shall see the best of the best battle for their lives!" yelled the king, unaware that he need not speak so loudly.

The crowd clapped joyously and we departed in the wee hours of the morning. Much to my relief, I was led back to the luscious bed and dropped off to sleep like a rock. Tomorrow would be the worst day yet, but all I could think about was sleep.

The screeching of the iron gate as it lifted over me felt otherworldly. A guard had to shove me to get me moving. Dumbly I walked into the arena. The glass man nodded to me as we each faced our opponents grimly. I took on a huge furry man while the glass man faced a genderless serpentine being.

The night before, it had become very clear that no alliances would be made. These two refused to speak with me or anyone else. The glass man consoled me, saying they were trying to make the ensuing fight easier on their conscience, it was easier to see me as an opponent than a friend. As we fought, I still persisted in trying to persuade him, but he merely ignored my pleas and tried to bash me with his club again and again. Golden arcs like my axe burst forth, making impact that much more powerful. Successfully I nimbly evaded each attack but it was becoming tiring. Backed into a corner, I was forced to use Tyler to slice his shins and roll out of the way of his club. It shattered the wall like nothing. My legs felt shaky as the ground quaked with every blow of his club. "Keep it together, Jane." I whispered to try and encourage myself. Around us, the soundtrack of riotous cries made the scene more intense. Trying to tune it out, I turned my attention to the task at hand. The club smashed a pillar to pebbles and I barely jumped away unscathed but tumbled into the line of fire of the glass man. The serpent lunged at me for an easy kill, wrapping its tail around my legs and hurling me to the ground. My head spun on impact and my shoulder and back screamed in pain but my arm remained free and I used my axe to slice its head clean off. It flew through the air, spraying blood and poison and the crowd went wild, thirsty for more killing. It landed with a wet thud. The furry giant used the opportunity to try and squish me like a bug. Just as he raised the club above his head a huge glass shard pierced his chest. The club slipped from his grasp. I glanced up to see the glass man use the giant's own club to smash his head in. I couldn't watch the gory scene and looked away. My hand held the axe in a viselike grip.

The glass man untangled me from the serpent's tail and picked me up, setting me on my feet.

I shook my head. "Kill me. I won't kill you. I won't." No tears threatened but I was unable to lift the axe. Whether he liked it or not I had decided he was my friend and nothing would move me to kill him.

He knelt on his knees before me, a half-smile lighting his face. "My name is Ajal." His hand came around to reveal a dagger. My dagger. Somehow, he'd gotten Lynn from my belt and before I could reach him, he stabbed himself in the chest and a sickening crack followed before he shattered into a million pieces.

Half the crowd cheered at a winner while the others seemed disappointed in such a humane death.

I felt sick to my stomach. What kind of race rejoiced in violence? In death?

Guards with hooks came out again and began hauling the bodies away, just like yesterday. I stood there, immobile, hands clenched around my axe. Tears streamed unbidden down my face. My eyes never left the pile of what used to be Ajal. Something in me snapped when a guard flung a large piece of glass into the cart, like it was garbage. My hands tightened their grip on the axe. I stroked the weapon through the air, left and right, watching in smug satisfaction as massive golden arcs swept up and down the arena, blowing everything in its path to smithereens. These aliens were monsters and deserved to die. Ferociously, I swung and swung, not even caring if the whole place came down upon me. But then something hit me from behind and everything went dark.

CHAPTER ELEVEN

I awoke with a pounding headache, a goose-egg on my noggin and all my belongings missing. I was back in my trusty cold cell. Chains bound my wrists, neck, and ankles. A little overkill, but I guess that was the punishment for ruining their precious games.

The door swung open with a bang and several guards awaited outside.

"Where are we going?" I asked.

The guard who unchained my neck responded, albeit rudely: "The king summoned you."

Silently, they led me up from the dungeons, past gardens and gaudily decorated rooms. Everyone we walked past grew silent, giving me angry glares. It would seem everyone was aware of my transgression. We came to a door with gold symbols carved into it and I knew the king must be on the other side.

They sat me on a chair clearly meant for an Ares, I felt like a child sitting in it. Taking in the room's grandeur, I quickly realized what this was: a courtroom. The king sat as judge, jury, and executioner. Ares dressed in white robes stood about him as his advisors but I knew better, what King Memign said would go unchallenged.

"What is your name?"

"Jane Aleah Prescott."

The man who had asked me wrote it on a tablet. He asked me many mundane questions, such as age, height, and so on. Finally, when he was finished, the king impatiently brushed him aside and began questioning me.

"Do you understand what your weapons are?"

I blanked suddenly, feeling like I was in Grade Three Science again. It was so obvious and yet I felt like he was trapping me.

Choosing the sarcastic route, I rolled my eyes. "Six daggers and an axe," I dryly stated.

He chuckled but wasn't amused. "Better question, are you aware of how you summon the power to fuel your weapons?"

I shrugged. "It just comes to me."

His eyes sparkled with excitement. It was quite disturbing and I shifted uncomfortably in my chair.

"It just comes to you," he repeated breathlessly. "How interesting."

The advisors grouped around him all murmured and one particularly tall man bent forward to whisper in the king's ear.

"Jane Aleah Prescott, I'm sure you are wondering why you are here. Let me get straight to the point. We have been searching for a warrior such as you to create a whole new breed of Ares! The games were an easy way to please my subjects, myself included," the men around him chuckled in agreement, "but their true purpose was to find one particular fighter who stood out among the rest. It has taken so long but finally, you're here!" Everyone in the room clapped and actually smiled at me as if I'd done something amazing.

I blinked in confusion. "I don't understand."

The king sat back. "Many years ago, I realized we could revolutionize our troops if only I found the correct," he paused searching for the right word, "mother, as it were, and it became clear to me that they were not on Trireme. So, we scoured galaxies, taking over planet after planet, plucking out only the greatest warriors from each and placing them in our great tournament. The winners are then used to make the army's next generation even greater than the last. But you, you are truly a delightful specimen."

The hairs on the back of my neck stood on end. Specimen? I stopped him before he could continue. "Are you saying you've killed billions of people, committed genocides, all in hopes to make your army that much better?" My question was met with silence. I nearly shouted. "When will it be enough?" I exhaled trying to calm my temper. It wouldn't do to lose my temper and be killed after Ajul sacrificed himself so that I might live.

King Memign grew serious. "When we defeat our mortal enemies, the Eirene," the king nearly spat.

Everyone present in the room grumbled their complaints and agreement.

"For centuries we have been locked in battle with that forsaken race. But with you," his eyes lit up again, "we could change the tide of the war."

"The Ares you sent to Earth, they were the last generation?"

"Yes. I thought they would win for sure with their sharp claws and speed. The man was from Lypimenos, a wonderful species. That generation excelled at taking over planets, we've used them for years, but sadly, against the Eirenites," his voice grew hard, "he was a disappointment. Just like all the others. I have high hopes for you."

"What of your tournament?" I asked curtly.

The king seemed mildly annoyed. "You practically destroyed my arena and everyone in it. It will have to be put on hold until we acquire more contestants."

"Seeing as I've won, am I also to be your concubine now?" Sarcasm protected me from the sheer horror and disgust I felt at the thought of us touching intimately.

King Memign laughed. "Of course not! That was just a front to our real cause. I feel as though our search is over!"

I swallowed. "But I'm not even that powerful! You said so yourself you gave me these powers. Even now I'm helpless without my weapons."

King Memign tapped his fingers on the table lightly. "That is only half-true."

What?

My mind blanked. What was he going on about now?

"The Sphygmos, or pulse of energy we sent to… Earth was it? It reacted with your body. Even we don't know why, but our beasts recognized the scent in the initial siege and didn't kill you." I recalled the two-horn who let me mysteriously live. "You are the one emotionally connected to your weapons thus giving them power, not I. Worry not, there are also a series of tests we need you to perform. Endurance, stamina, and the brute strength of your weapons which we wish to recreate."

My weapons in the hands of the Ares? No. It couldn't happen. I'd rather die that let that happen. Perhaps I could hang myself on my chains or stop eating. Trying not to panic, I breathed slowly. Maybe there was some way I could buy myself time. "Once you defeat the Eirene, will the tournaments stop?"

He replied immediately. "Of course not."

I responded with equal speed. "Then I refuse."

He smiled deeply, revealing dimples. "My dear girl, this is not a question of if you're willing or not." Without waiting for a reply, he shouted a myriad of orders to everyone in the room. "Prepare a feast in honour of my triumph, chain her to the pillars in the great hall and awaken the queen. She will want to know of this day's great success!"

CHAPTER TWELVE

My feet were sore from standing so long and my wrists bore black bruises from the tall chains lifting my arms above me. The Ares partied until late into the evening. Men and woman came to gawk, touch, and speak to me. Anything to get a reaction. Now I knew how the Queen's Life Guards felt. To everyone I remained the same: a stoic silent creature.

Queen Jezebel, a very tall lady with long black hair and striking clothes, condescended to come meet me. Upon closer inspection, I realized she was extremely tall, even taller than the king. It was becoming clear to me that height went a long way with the Ares in social aspects.

"Sweet child, I hear you are the key to our victory?"

I could hear the disdain despite her gracious smile. No amount of makeup or beauty treatments could make this woman beautiful. The queen's eyes were a jaundiced colour and full of hate. Instantly, I wondered just who wore the crown in this relationship.

"So I hear," I replied, speaking a little louder so she might hear me above the dinner guests.

"Hmm. I hope so. Aren't you aware of what we do to candidates who fail?"

I was in a morbid, angry mood and this queen wasn't helping. "Burn them in oil and send the remaining body parts home?"

Her fake smile deepened. "Close. But if you're taking requests, I'll make sure to pass it along."

I smiled sweetly. "You do that." If you're gonna go you might as well go big, right?

Queen Jezebel sauntered away and I focused my attention back on my feet.

Soon after, the king quieted his guests and began a drunken ramble about his successes and so on but soon his list of triumphs turned to me and my ears perked.

"...with great power, which we all witnessed yestermorning," he was saying, and the crowd murmured in agreement. "However! While we acknowledge her strength and our need of it, the death of so many Ares cannot go unpunished. Therefore, my advisors and I have decided on the Almourrian Rite of Passage, which will serve as both punishment and will evaluate her endurance."

Whoops and cheers arose from the crowded room. Punishment? He'd mentioned none of that in our little meeting!

Two guards removed my chains from the pillars and purposefully led me through the crowded room, clearly in display for all to see. Huge crimson curtains lined the walls. One of the men escorting me pulled them back to reveal invisible glass windows. Trireme was hovering very near the surface of a planet, one that was clearly not Earth.

The king and queen gloated over me.

"Jane Aleah Prescott, you shall serve your sentence for one week. If you survive on your own in this desert, you shall be rewarded with being the mother of the next Ares army."

King Memign nodded to the guard standing next to me who promptly unshackled my wrists and forced me to my knees while facing the ominous door. A metallic ring sounded behind me but I dared not peek. The room was eerily silent and in the reflection of the glass I saw the queen raise a massive broadsword. Without hesitation she sliced it across my back. I stifled a scream, biting my lip instead.

Doubling over I forced air into my lungs. Hot blood seeped down my back, staining my shirt. The dusty desert down below would not help me heal. The door opened and a cool breeze brushed my cheek. How I had missed fresh air.

King Memign suddenly grabbed me and personally shoved me out the door. Once outside, I realized the great hall had removed itself from Trireme, like the ship itself were extending an arm, and that we weren't that high off the ground. Still, I landed on my right leg funny and a great pain erupted there. Quickly I rolled to my front, but sand had already crept into the wound.

Tears slid down my face, the first since returning to my destroyed home. How was I to get out of this? I would die here, and if I lived, death awaited me with the Ares, Queen Jezebel would make sure of it.

I sat unmoving for a time, contemplating.

No.

I would find a way. This was a whole planet; surely, I could hide from the Ares.

Feeling encouraged, I slowly sat up. The night air kept me cool. Ripping off excess fabric I tried to wrap it around my wound as best I could. When I was satisfied, I forced myself to stand. First, I needed to find water and something to defend myself with in case I wasn't alone. I scanned the horizon in every direction. Nothing but barren desert. Fine, no worries, I'd just walk and see where I ended up.

CHAPTER THIRTEEN

My knee was throbbing, as were my back and my head. I hurt everywhere and all I wanted was a dark, comfortable place to sleep. The strange looking sun had lit up several hours before and I had only then realized the sand was a bleak black ash heap stretching for miles ahead of me. Everything was flat sand; not a single sign of any life or anything was in sight. Still, I forced myself to hobble along. At least the weather hovered around the same pleasant temperature with that cool, albeit dry, breeze.

I was unable to determine how much time had passed, as the light in the sky didn't move, but I knew it had to at least be a few hours. My good leg ached from carrying all my weight while the other throbbed in agony. The wound on my back felt crusty and sore. If I moved the wrong way, I could feel blood ooze out and the sickening feel of skin moving in a way it shouldn't. All I could think about was water and how dry my mouth was; it even trumped my rumbling stomach.

Feeling faint, I opted to try sitting down. Perhaps it was best to travel by night and rest during the day. I squinted up at the sun. What was it? It didn't hurt to look at and yet it lit everything up as brightly as Earth's sun, not to mention it didn't burn my skin, yet when I shut my eyes, its warmth could be clearly felt. Where was I?

The black sand went on endlessly. There were no trees or buildings or wildlife. Perhaps the elements would kill me. Still, it was better than the Ares creating killing machines out of my DNA.

I sat and sat until the light began to dim. Stiffly and very slowly, I hoisted myself upright and began walking. After several hours, as I stumbled along, I noticed to my left were what looked like trees. Excitement fuelled my legs to hobble forward, even though my pace was a fraction of what it could be. Sure enough, there was a forest and mountains up ahead. It was really quite beautiful, not that I had much time to care or notice. I estimated it was probably about an hour to the tree line where it would be easy to find water and shelter. My foot hit something in the sand and I collapsed on my face. A groan escaped my lips and I lay still trying to catch my breath. The pain refused to subside; how was I to endure this?

When I finally regained my footing, I was dizzy and the treeline looked fuzzy. Perhaps I should make the trees in daylight... But then the hairs on the back of my neck stood on end and I felt like someone was watching me.

I forced one foot in front of the other but tripped again on something hard. In the dark I could hear the sand slide as someone walked near. I held my breath. I had no weapons on me and hoped the creature stalking me was friendly. I heaved myself up and walked forward again and for a time everything was silent. Perhaps they were gone? The tip of a blade on my neck stopped me dead in my tracks.

"Halt!" the male voice cried.

"I've halted," I said immediately then bit my tongue.

His tone was suspicious and harsh. "So you have. Who are you? Why are you here?"

I struggled to keep my eyes open and white dots filled my vision. I could not faint now, of all times. "I am Jane... The Ares..." I hesitated, how could I finish that sentence? "The Ares sent me here as punishment." My voice cracked with my throat begging for water.

The tip of his blade disappeared from my neck and a light illuminated from his pocket, shining more than enough light for each of us to survey one another.

His eyes widened slightly at the sight of me and so did mine. This man was a hunk, easily six foot three with dark hair and eyes to match. His bare arms were tattooed as was his face, although only a little. They looked like tribal markings.

"Why did they punish you?"

The white dots clouding my vision grew and everything was blurry and suddenly I couldn't determine up from down. I was falling forward and the stranger caught me.

"Excuse me..." I mumbled.

The man chuckled. "You are excused."

The last thing I remembered was his shock at my wounds and him hoisting me over his shoulder like a wild hog, then everything went black.

CHAPTER FOURTEEN

P eeling my eyes open, I squinted at the world around
me. The dredges of a nightmare still hung about
me. I felt like I hadn't slept a wink. Too scared to
move, I studied my room from the uncomfortable position
of lying on my stomach. Vines and leaves grew up the
wall, the bed I was in was massive and one wall was
completely open, overlooking thick plants and a beautiful
view of waterfalls. A gentle breeze wafted in and I heard
voices from the hall.

The same man from the night before entered and I
had to check myself because he was even more handsome
in daylight.

"You're awake."

I bit back a sarcastic response and nodded.

"Let me help you move so you can eat and drink."

Before I could blink the stranger had his arms around
me, rolled me over and had me sitting comfortably against
a wall of pillows.

Despite his best efforts, contact on my back and knees
sent shooting pain up and down my body. Grimacing, I
still managed to thank him.

He gave me a sympathetic smile while handing me a clay cup of clear water. "So, Jane, what did you do that upset the Ares enough to banish you here?"

It bothered me that I didn't know his name. The man sat on the edge of my bed, clearly comfortable in the space. He looked at me expectantly, patiently waiting for my response.

I downed the cup. "I killed some of King Memign's citizens."

Shock lit up his face and excitement fuelled his words. "You did? How many?"

My eyelids felt heavy and the cup slipped out of my hand shattering on the floor. Fighting to stay awake I frowned thinking of the water. "Did you drug me?"

He looked sheepish. "Yes. You weren't sleeping well and I didn't think you'd drink it so fast."

I scoffed weakly. "I don't even know your name…"

He smiled revealing an adorable dimple. "Cade."

My eyes closed of their own volition. My last view was Cade pulling the quilts over me.

When I woke, I was breathing hard and rivulets of sweat dotted my brow. The room was dark. I guessed the nightmare of reliving my family's death in new grotesque ways still lingered despite the sleeping drug.

Slowly slipping out of bed, I hobbled to the open wall, drinking in fresh air. My back stung but my knee was doing surprisingly well. The bandage on my arm had also been freshly changed.

I guessed it had been two days since the Ares plunked me on this planet. How could I escape? I didn't want to put these people in danger.

I limped to the entrance of my room and found a twisted hallway guarded by two armed men. The lavatory also lacked a door; it, too, had an elongated hall.

"These people don't have doors?" I asked aloud.

Never mind, I'd just slip out the massive open wall. I contemplated drinking water before I left but didn't trust it to be drug free.

The ledge was only three feet high and I scrambled down. Now it was just a matter of left or right. Left look thick with brush while right led to more building.

"Left it is," I muttered beginning the trek.

A broken branch would have been perfect as a makeshift crutch but scanning the forest floor proved impossible in the dark. It was slow going with my knee now throbbing and a headache beginning to form. Plus, my stomach growled angrily and there was still my back, but I persisted.

Distantly, I could hear shouts as the light in the sky finally began to glow. Had they found me missing? I hurried along because I felt I'd taken the obvious escape route. Sooner or later I'd come to the desert, right?

All too soon, I burst through the trees where a bunch of early risers were taking a bath in a pristine lake. Some looked shocked at my appearance while others didn't even notice I was there.

Just as I began asking directions, three guards popped out of the trees. Dread fell in the pit of my stomach. I was caught, there was no way I could outrun them in my condition and taking a hostage was out of the question. A spear in the back didn't bode well.

To my surprise they looked more anxious than angry. "Miss Jane, please return with us. You are not well."

Did I really have a choice? Perhaps I was hasty in my escape…maybe I wasn't a prisoner after all?

In the end, my stomach won out and I agreed to return. Plus, the men looked uncomfortable speaking to me in front of a dozen half naked women and I was feeling gracious.

CHAPTER FIFTEEN

The room I'd left remained the same save the bed was made and a steaming tray of breakfast lay in wait. Unceremoniously, I delved into the meal and had barely finished when a man came to summon me.

Cade was on the roof atop a stone bench overlooking the city, lost in thought.

The servant left us alone and it was a long while before he spoke to me. "Do you feel unsafe here?" His eyes never left the stunning view of the waterfalls and mist.

I pondered before answering. "No."

Cade gave no response.

"Forgive my escape attempt. I suppose the hospitality of the Ares has put me on edge."

After a short pause he finally smiled and turned to me. "I can understand that."

A funny thought hit me. "How can you understand me?" Surely the Ares hadn't put communication chips in these people as well?

Cade's brow furrowed curiously. "We're speaking English."

"You speak English?"

"Obviously."

Clearly humans were very close-minded about aliens. "Well, then." Trying to brush off my embarrassment I continued. "Where am I?" I asked attempting to change the subject.

"This is Almourr." He gestured to the city below. "Almourr used to be a great bountiful planet until the Ares tried conquering us."

"The whole planet was jungle?"

Cade nodded. "The Ares… burnt everything to ash. Fortunately, we won, though barely. This is all that's left. Slowly, we've been rebuilding and replanting our lush forests."

Staring off into the distance I felt sad. For Almourr and Ewer and Earth… But then I realized the answer was right in my grasp. There was hope for Earth yet.

"How did you beat the Ares?"

Cade looked intrigued. "I'll tell you if you answer some of my questions."

"Agreed." I had nothing to hide.

"This entire planet was lush untamed jungle, the natural enemy of the lower-class Ares. But instead of sending the upperclassmen, they sent the lower, underestimating our jungle. Many did not survive while the others could barely find our cities. Ironically, after all their efforts were spent, they found we were not biologically fitted to their DNA codes, therefore we could not become the mother of their army. After learning that, they admitted defeat and left us in peace." He turned back to face the exquisite scenery. "Well, that is until they throw prisoners like you to die in our desert."

"Not biologically fitted?" I asked.

"Yes. They sent a pulse of electric energy to try and knock out our power but our power is botanically based so it was completely ineffective."

"How?"

"The Beacon in the sky is actually a large plant that is bioluminescent. The same goes for all our lamps and lights."

I stared at the light in the sky; no wonder it didn't move across the sky.

"Fascinating."

"The light affects our DNA and makes it incompatible with the Ares and as such we cannot birth the Ares army. They had no more reason to try and take over, and we put up more of a fight than they liked."

I felt at a loss. The advantage of power matched with the harsh jungle terrain helped the Almourrians win.

"Your weapons pierce the skin of the, lower-class, you called it?"

Cade looked surprised. "Easily. Wounds with their own claws are the only way to kill them. It was very difficult to catch the first one." His eyes widened at the memory. "We also had to prevent them from stampeding in a horde."

"But how did you remove the claws? I found it impossible."

Cade seemed confused. "Perhaps the metal blades on Almourr are sharper? It took some time but eventually we could saw through the skin. Once we had one, we had them all."

I felt the gears working in my head. With Cade's help, Earth might still have a fighting chance. But how to convince him? "In your opinion can Earth, my home planet, survive?"

A darkness crept over his face. "They took you away to play in their games, yes?" I nodded, scared of what he was trying to say. "Then Earth has a week. At most. Then they will completely destroy Earth and add its ruins to the great empire of Trireme."

I leaned back on the bench staring at the city below but not seeing anything. I asked a question I knew the answer to. "Is there any way the Almourrians would be willing to fight for Earth?"

Cade patted my hand sympathetically. "Even if there were, is there anyone left to fight for?" His voice was low and gentle and I thought back to the horde that attacked the safe camp. It was highly doubtful that many survived.

I was aware of Cade watching me, willing me to look at him. Slowly, I turned towards him with watery eyes. "Still. If there is even one person I have to try and save them." Pulling my hand out of his grasp I stood up. "How can I sneak back on to Trireme?"

"Surely you can't be serious?" he cried.

I glared down at him, my sorrow turning to anger fueling my will to fight. "I am perfectly serious," I spat.

"It's too dangerous. You can't!"

I could have laughed. "I'll need my weapons if I'm going to fight."

Cade stood up looming over me. "I cannot tell you. It's suicide!"

I felt my face heat. "Fine. Be a coward! But if I can't sneak in, I'll just wait for them to come pick me up." I spun on my heel and left Cade to lick his wounds. How dare he tell me what to do. Of course, it would be dangerous but this was genocide! The whole human population would be utterly destroyed, if it wasn't already, and I had to see, to make sure I wasn't the last one.

CHAPTER SIXTEEN

Knowing I wasn't a prisoner made walking out the front door all too easy. I was still in a considerable amount of pain but being angry sure helped.

As I walked through the city, it became clear to me that the Almourrians had no need for any real transportation and were quite primitive people. The market was bustling was activity. Vendors sold fresh fruit, fabrics, spices, and all manner of pottery. Everyone around was haggling. I noticed a vendor selling books and inquired if Almourrians had any spaceships.

"Not from around here, are you, miss?" he asked, staring at my arms

I realized that I was the only one in the square whose arms didn't bear tattoos. Self-consciously, I rubbed them and leaned back. "No. And I do need to get off-planet." There was a sentence I never thought I'd say. "Do you know of anyone who could help me?"

The fellow had kind eyes and leaned in close as if to tell me a secret. "The only person with those resources is the king. King Edgarr."

"Where can I find him?"

"The palace, of course."

I looked to the heavens for patience. "Where can I find the palace, then?"

He gave me directions and I found myself in the center of the city, in front of a huge building that surrounded a massive green trunk that trailed high into the sky. It had to be the Beacon for the light seemed to be at emanating from the top.

How did one go about meeting a king? I paced back and forth at the entrance until a guard came up to me thus interrupting my worry session.

"Anything I can do for you, miss?"

I smiled nervously. "Yes, I'd like to book an appointment with the king. It's quite urgent."

He smiled. "Yes. Right this way."

I was led to a balding, short man with tattoos covering his arms. "The king is free to meet with you…?"

"Jane Prescott." I finished for him.

"Miss Jane, tomorrow morning for tea. How does that sound?"

I bit my lip. It would have to do. Sleeping in the forest should be like second nature by now but with my wounds, it would prove difficult. No matter. I wouldn't let Cade get in the way of my plans. "Yes. That would be lovely."

Wandering through the town to see the sights seemed like a lovely idea until my knee throbbed, my head ached, and sweat moistened my back. I absolutely could not get sick. People needed me. I sat by a fountain to catch my breath and people-watch. I realised, quite quickly, Almourrians weren't so different from humans. Men walked briskly through the streets. Kids played a version of soccer while their mothers did laundry. Even the young ones had tattoos; perhaps they were birthmarks.

"I heard you got an audience with King Edgarr, very impressive."

I jumped despite myself and promptly rolled my eyes. "Cade, go away. I'm still angry with you."

"Angry or not, you still need to eat and drink water. Come, you do not look well."

I wiped my damp forehead with the back of my hand. I knew he was right but didn't want to go with him.

"I'm sorry I offended you, but please, come with me. You need to get well enough to see the king."

"You're helping me?"

He sighed. "You have a better chance if you sneak aboard Trireme instead of them recapturing you. But first you have to convince the king to lend you a ship."

Swallowing my pride, I allowed him to help me up and together, we made our way back to his home.

Dinner was quiet and peaceful and Cade convinced me to join him on the roof for some advice and terabaska juice... Whatever that was.

The night was warm and stars glittered brilliantly above. I could grow old in this peaceful haven. I blushed at the implications of my own thoughts.

"Are you well? You look flushed."

I had to look away suddenly afraid he could read my mind. "I am. I am fine. Maybe some water?"

He poured me a glass and we sat overlooking the city. Nothing could be heard but rustling leaves and animals that sounded similar to frogs and crickets. It struck me anew that I was on a whole new planet. Never in my life would I have guessed that.

"So if I leave tomorrow, that gives me a four-day head start."

Cade nodded and gently set his untouched drink on the table. "The tea tomorrow has certain guidelines they will expect you to follow."

I felt a nervous knot form in my stomach. "Certainly King Edgarr wouldn't let a genocide take place over improper etiquette?" I was saying it more for myself. He absolutely could if he saw fit.

"The king is old and favours protocol above flattery and gifts. The way to impress him and get in his good graces is etiquette."

I groaned. I wasn't stupid enough to think Earth's table etiquette was the same as that of Almourr. "But I don't know anything about Almourr!"

Cade smiled and that incredibly adorable dimple returned. "I'll teach you."

Hours must have passed and trying to remember everything was becoming difficult. Some things were the same such as no elbows on the table and teacups were still on saucers, but everything from there went sideways. I was not to sit directly in front of the king as that was rude and I was not to reach for anything. I would have a personal attendant whom I was expected to order about as would everyone else in attendance. And speaking of, the new first prince of Almourr would also be present, as he was learning from his father the trade of becoming king. Then there was the mumbo jumbo of spoons, knives, and forks to remember. And the three bowls I would be using, and how I was expected to leave a few bites on the plate. Finishing was ever so rude as it 'conveyed a gluttonous stomach and an eagerness to depart'.

"And Miss Jane, you must alter your status. I am afraid the king will think less of you if you are just a commoner from Earth."

"But that *is* what I am. Earth has several countries all with different political powers. There are several different royal families."

"You mean more than one king?"

"Yes!" I felt a swell of pride at his amazement. "Earth is quite large."

Cade rubbed his fuzzy chin. "How about ambassador of Earth? That wouldn't be a lie, you are here to speak on their behalf. And you were handpicked by the Ares to be the mother of their race, you must be special."

"I was thinking we leave that part out, actually."

"It's no good." Cade was shaking his head. "King Edgarr will want to know how you got here. If you say you crashed, he'll want to find the wreckage. Besides, your military feats might impress him. Almourrians do not prejudice against female warriors as some places do."

I conceded. "Fine. So, is that all?"

"No. You need proper attire."

"Tea ceremonies are a big deal," I said dejectedly.

"Yes, but the uniforms can be quite lovely." Cade pulled a box from beneath his chair and held it out to me. I opened the box and smiled as I lifted the dress out. It was a beautiful cream coloured gown that went below my knees, a classy length. It was trimmed in red and had a high neck line. There was a long wide shimmery see-through red scarf that I was told would be draped over the front and hang down my back. The ends were stitched with dark red that complemented the ensemble.

"Where did you get this?" I asked breathlessly. I was almost excited to wear it.

Cade avoided the subject. "Tea-time is two hours past the Beacon lighting, maids will come to assist you. Shall I walk you to your room?"

He held out his hand for me. It would seem he noticed my fatigue before me and I accepted, allowing him to guide me back to my room.

Cade seemed to linger at the hall that led to my room.

"Is everything okay?" I asked curiously.

He nodded but a frown remained fixated on his face.

"What's the matter?" I pressed.

"I've just been wondering now, what does sexy mean?"

I stuttered and my mind blanked. Was he trying to hit on me?

"You said I was sexy when I first saved you," he explained. "Don't you remember?"

My eyes got huge. Did I say that? Out loud? "It, uh, it means... Huge."

"Huge?" He cocked a brow and for a second I almost thought he was teasing me but then he was all innocence again.

"Yes. Like a huge person. Not like fat! You aren't fat... Like, tall. I must have been speaking gibberish. I was delirious after all."

His eyebrows rose and he nodded. "Oh, okay then. I'm glad I cleared that up, I might've said you were sexy and looked the fool."

I knew I was blushing hard now. "Yes. Well. Goodnight." I practically ran through the hall into my room. What a mortifying conversation! I touched my cheeks several minutes later and they were still hot to touch. What an aggravating man!

CHAPTER SEVENTEEN

The next morning, I awoke in the dark with maids hovering about my bed. Like any normal human, I yelped in fear but then the morning flowers bloomed in my room bringing exquisite light to all corners of the space and I recognized who they were.

"Gracious, you guys scared me."

"Forgive us, milady," replied a maid named Everest, "we only wished to wake you peacefully."

"Were all six of you necessary?" I retorted.

The younger maids were clearly amused but were doing their best to hide it.

As expected, the dress fit like a glove but with wiggle room for the bandages on my back. Again, I was impressed with Cade's planning. My hair was pinned tightly back into a neat bun and they dressed it up with large red flowers and tiny cream ones.

"May I say, you look stunning," breathed the youngest girl, Margot.

I gave a quick thanks before they ushered me to the front entrance. Cade awaited to escort me. He looked all dressed up too, in a deep blue jacket that fitted him very nicely. I had to deliberately stop myself from staring and he seemed not to notice my getup.

"We must be right on time. Early is desperate, late is indifferent. More suited for a social calling," he reminded me for the fiftieth time as we walked to the center of town.

"You're making me nervous," I chided.

Cade smiled. "You need not be. King Edgarr is a sympathetic man."

"What about the prince? If he is advising the king, doesn't that mean I also need to win his vote?"

Cade smiled. "Perhaps. But an advisor is just that. He cannot make the final decision. You just have to make sure your argument is more convincing than his."

I sighed under my breath. "No pressure."

We were greeted at the entrance by the same man I spoke to yesterday and Cade and I parted ways.

"The king wishes to have tea in the garden. You are a touch early but no matter, His Highness detests waiting."

I willed my heart to calm down. I'd rather look desperate than uncaring. Perhaps the punctual king would feel bad for making me wait.

The gardens were exquisite. It was the perfect balance of untamed nature with calculated shrubs and flowers placed just so. Everything was so green and vibrant. I was beginning to love this place. The Beacon in the sky was brightly glowing now setting the place under a warm filter of light.

The table was set with several bowls and cutlery just as Cade had explained. How I wished he could be here to help me through this.

I stood at the table waiting for Kind Edgarr. Cade told me not to sit before the king unless he offered, so there I stood going over every last detail in my head.

"Good morning," a chipper voice called through the garden. I turned to see an ancient man hobbling his way toward me. If not for the rich robes and crown atop his head I would never have guessed this man was the king. His body was failing but his eyes betrayed a lively soul, probably prone to mischief.

"Good morning, King Edgarr." Reminding myself not to bow, I took his hand and kissed the royal seal tattooed there, as was proper.

The king was surprised and his smiled reached his eyes. "You may sit. My son is running late so we shall wait for him but fret not, I am told he is arriving."

Both of us sat and naught could be heard but birds twittering overhead and the rustle of our clothes as we sat.

A minute of silence passed before the king slammed his hand on the table causing me to jump. "Bah! Let us wait no further."

Each of us began asking our attendants for tea and treats until finally they stepped back to allow us to talk.

"My girl, what is your name? And where do you hail from?"

"I am Jane Prescott and I am from Earth."

The king looked neither surprised nor too interested, not the most encouraging start but I pressed on. "Shall we discuss why I asked to meet with you?"

The king smiled and waved his hand, urging me to continue.

"Earth is in trouble. Nearly three years ago, the Ares attacked my planet and I was recently chosen as Earth's champion to fight in their tournament." I swallowed, wishing for water. "I won the tournament through pure luck, but King Memign and his queen still named me to be mother of the next generation of Ares warriors."

The king set his cup down and leaned forward; that had caught his attention.

"But they sent me here as punishment and now all I ask is if I could borrow one of your ships so I can sneak aboard Trireme and get my weapons back. Then I can try and save Earth before it is destroyed."

I stayed silent anxiously awaiting his answer. The man was impossible to read. "Why did they send you here as punishment?"

"I cannot say why, they chose Almourr, not I."

King Edgarr laughed and I realized my silly error. A blush heated my cheeks. "Forgive me, I misunderstood. I killed Ares citizens and was therefore punished."

The king's spoon clattered on the table, his response mirroring Cade's. "You did? How many?"

"Hundreds, sir. I destroyed King Memign's arena and almost everyone in it."

King Edgarr slapped his hand on the table again and laughed gleefully. "Wonderful!" His smile settled my rattling nerves. This was going well.

"Forgive me for being so late, father."

King Edgarr sobered up quite quickly. "You may sit. Miss Jane, this is the newly first prince of Almourr, Cade Edgarr."

Son of a bitch!

I bit my tongue to keep the words in my mind only. He was the first prince but didn't tell me? Suspicion twisted my gut. Was Cade actually not on my side? I could barely comprehend the conversation father and son were having. The king was filling him in on all my feats so far but Cade looked far from impressed.

He turned to me and introduced us to each other. It was clear Cade meant to pretend we had never met before this moment.

"What says you, my son, shall we lend her a ship?" King Edgarr focused all his attention on Cade, completely emotionless.

Cade turned to me. "What do you intend to do with our ship?"

"Just get aboard Trireme and steal my weapons back."

Cade frowned. "Weapons?"

"Yes. I will need them if I ever hope to save Earth."

"So you want to assassinate King Memign? Cutting off the head of the snake as it were?"

My hands went cold. To be honest I hadn't gotten that far in my plan. It would be a miracle if I made it that far. I didn't even know where my weapons would be kept. I cleared my throat. "I intend to do whatever is necessary to save what is left of my home."

Cade's brows furrowed more. "You sound like the Ares. With nothing on your mind but war."

I looked to King Edgarr for help but he offered nothing. "Sirs, we have a common enemy. I merely wish to prevent genocide. The Almourrians survived! Please, give us humans a chance to as well."

"We *barely* survived," Cade said quietly, an angry edge to his voice and I suddenly wondered why he was newly the first prince.

"Barely surviving is better than not at all. Please, you have nothing to lose!"

Cade sat back, eyebrows raised. "Nothing to lose? If the Ares find out you used one of our ships to sneak aboard, they will name us an accomplice and finally finish us off."

"The Ares will be here in four days to collect me. Will they not also be angry you took me in and fixed me up, hence ruining their examination of me? Their ever-so-precious mother?"

Cade's expression darkened. "Not if we offer you up."

I could have laughed. "You know as well as I that they will kill you all for good measure. It doesn't look good on their record that you remain an undefeated foe. If they use me and defeat the Eirene it is doubtless, they will set their sights for Almourr. King Memign is too proud to let you live."

King Edgarr leaned forward, his happy tone breaking the tense atmosphere. "Well, there you have it. It would seem our only strategy is to attack before they do. Miss Jane, you may have our ship but I cannot ask any of my men to accompany you."

Before I could agree Cade interjected. "There is no need father because I found a volunteer."

Clearly unhappy at the thought of sending a young woman into battle alone the king's face brightened. "Who is it, my son?"

"Me."

The king and I shared the same expression. After this little tea session, I found Cade to be extremely dull looking and a complete arse.

"Absolutely not," King Edgarr growled.

"Yeah, not in a million years," I echoed.

"Yes, but we can't wait that long, we have only four days, remember?"

I rolled my eyes.

The king scoffed. "Cade, I cannot allow this! You are to assume the throne, with no heir, might I remind you. You simply cannot go rampaging through space to fulfill a personal vendetta! There are responsibilities here to take care of." I suddenly felt out of place in this argument but King Edgarr wasn't finished. "And what would people say of you escorting a single woman alone? For who knows how long?"

"Actually, father, this woman is my fiancée."

I choked on my tea. What nonsense was he spouting now?

The king eyed me suspiciously. "But she cannot marry you! She simply isn't eligible."

"Father," Cade chided softly, "it's the Modern Century, surely you can make an exception. Besides, she is an ambassador of Earth and an exceptional warrior. Surely allying with Earth is suitable to you?"

"Well actually, you can't ally with any one person to ally with…"

Cade cut me off and patted my hand as though we were a couple. "Hush now, darling, the men are talking."

I swore I wouldn't lose my top but suddenly I was standing and shouting. "Are all men stupid?! I am perfectly capable of handling myself out there, thank you very much! I don't need your help, you pampered prince!"

The king looked utterly shocked and Cade rose swiftly to his feet and circled his arm around me. "Now, now, my lady. No need to get so upset. You see, father, she is so spirited and I love her so dearly," he bopped me on the nose as he spoke, "that I cannot bear to let her go fight by herself. Nor do I trust any man to protect her."

I shoved him off me. "We are not engaged!"

The king looked completely speechless and turned to Cade. "Is this true?"

"By my honour as a prince we are. She accepted my hand when she stayed in my home unescorted for two consecutive nights and sealed it when she wore this piece of clothing given to her by me directly."

King Edgarr glanced at me. "Is that true?"

I stammered. "Well, yes... But I'm not Almourrian! Surely it doesn't count!"

The king sighed. "I'm sorry, Miss Jane, but by all accounts, you are engaged to my son and it is within his rights to protect you on your mission to Trireme." And turning to Cade, the jerk allowed him to come with me.

CHAPTER EIGHTEEN

"You! You are a horrible human being!"

Cade folded his arms. "I'm not a human."

I threw my hands up in the air. "You are infuriating!"

"Do you even know how to drive a spaceship?"

"Yes!" I bluffed. "Autopilot."

He actually had the gall to double over in laughter. I stood there tapping my foot impatiently. When he was finally done, he explained. "Jane, I orchestrated this whole thing. I knew my father would never let me go just because I wanted to."

"But all those things were true! Just how long have you been orchestrating?"

Cade rubbed the back of his neck. "Since I saw how determined you were to save Earth."

I inhaled deeply. "I am so incredibly angry with you right now."

"Look, you don't have to marry me for real."

It was my turn to laugh. "That was never going to happen, Cade! What I meant was the tea! Why did you put up such a fight if you were on my side?"

Cade put his hands behind his back. "Several reasons. I am the first prince of Almourr now and I have to do its people justice. I am going to be their protector. Soon." I thought of his aging father. Soon seemed an appropriate term. "And my father never would have believed my ruse if I just buckled under your pretty blue eyes."

Did he just say pretty? Focus, Jane focus! Choosing to ignore his compliment I told him to continue.

"Plus I really do want to go defeat the Ares. Once and for all. But I am sorry for manipulating you like that."

I sighed heavily, defeated. "Fine. But once we get to Trireme, we're splitting up. You go do what you need to and I will go find my weapons."

"You can't be serious."

"Oh, I am. We are clearly going for different reasons. I don't need to kill King Memign or his creepy wife I just need to get my weapons and stop them from destroying Earth."

Cade frowned. "I thought you were stopping it by killing the king and queen."

I shook my head. "I was speaking to your father after the tea and he explained the explosive device is already on Earth and will be detonated soon. Manually. Trireme has no control over the device. Once the Ares are finished, they'll destroy Earth, I have to dismantle the weapon first."

"Ah, the planet killer. And how do you expect to do that?"

I shrugged. "I don't know. But that's none of your concern. Once you drop me off at home, I'll find a way."

Cade looked at me with an expression I'd never seen before. It was either respect or pity, I couldn't decipher which.

"Your supplies are ready, sir."

The man interrupting was Cade's manservant. We separated to change into appropriate attire. The garments were neatly folded on the bed. What kind of place took accepting clothing as a sign of engagement? Not wanting to waste time, I grabbed them and rushed to get ready. Despite my speed, Cade still beat me and was waiting patiently at the entrance to his house.

He was fitted in black just like me, with guns and daggers on his person. The man looked good in black. The colour of his hair and eyes popped and somehow, the marking on his face made him look enticing. I needed a cold glass of water.

"Is everything okay? Your face is flushed."

I cleared my throat feigning calm. "Me? Oh yeah I'm just a little hot." I'd never felt this way about anyone, even Luke. What was the matter with me? After Luke, I'd sworn to be more careful and here I'd known the guy less than two days and he'd already manipulated me into being his fiancée.

Cade was nothing like Luke, I suddenly thought. Cade admitted to all his wrongs and apologized, Luke would never. And in the end, he was successful in getting me a ship.

We each had two bags to carry as we walked to the shipyard. Again, I was reminded at how amazing Almourr was. Cliffs jutted up above us and birds I could never have imagined flew up ahead. Water trickled down the stone walls and all the flowers glowed. Suddenly, I wished I could witness this place at night when the Beacon was dark and the evening blossoms lit up. A part of me would miss this wondrous jungle. What a simple life. I could retire here... If I wasn't supposed to marry the would-be king. The reminder made me frown and I smacked Cade.

"Ow! What was that for?"

I sniffed. "Everything."

We reached the docks, logged out the ship we were taking and headed to *The Exagora*. I didn't know anything about spaceships but it looked nice enough. Although it was nothing like the *Millennium Falcon* or the *Enterprise.* Each ship had its own docking station and magically hovered above ground. I had to stop myself from staring. These people weren't primitive at all, they had a whole fleet of ships!

A young man stood waiting for us in our station. He smiled brightly when he saw us. His bare arms boasted ring tattoos similar to Cade's, albeit significantly smaller ones.

"Hi, I'm Brigham. I was assigned by King Edgarr to accompany you as your chaperone."

Suddenly I found his smile fake and grating. I wanted to smack Cade again but on the face. With my fist.

Cade however, beat me to the punch. "Yes, I understand. Brigham, was it?" Without warning he punched Brigham and the man went out like a light. Cade graciously caught him and shoved him into a nearby supply closet.

"Cade!" I hissed. "What are you doing?"

He smiled devilishly. "I don't know about you, but I don't want a chaperone getting in the way."

My eyebrows could not go any higher. "We do not *need* a chaperone," I corrected.

Cade stood with three heavy boxes preparing to load our ship. "I don't think Brigham deserves to chaperone a fake couple on such a dangerous mission. Do you?"

I scuffed my shoe against the pavement. He *did* have a point. "Fine. But did you have to hit him?"

Cade rolled his eyes and mumbled something about delicacy and women. Choosing to pick my battles, I let it go. Today had been exhausting already and it was only the beginning.

We had been flying through endless darkness for an hour in utter silence and the beautiful faraway stars had become bland. I was going to go nuts. Out of the corner of my eye, I glanced at Cade and found him staring at me.

"What?" I asked turning to him.

He shrugged. "I'm bored."

"Me too." Fiddling with my fingers I worked up the courage to ask him about his title. "Cade," I cleared my throat before continuing. "I understand if you don't want to answer but why does everyone call you the *newly* first prince?"

"Oh. Well." He struggled to find the words. "I was the second prince but when the Ares attacked five years ago, they killed my older brother, making me the first prince. My three little sisters also were... They didn't make it."

I touched his arm sharing his pain. "I'm sorry," I whispered.

He smiled a little bit before returning the question. "Who did they take from you?"

Retracting my hands I folded them in my lap, squeezing them for support. I hadn't told anyone what happened except Harriet, and Ajul got the quick version. "It was Christmas and a two-horn, uh, the smallest of the lower-class, attacked and killed everyone. I found them in the kitchen." That was an understatement, I'd only found pieces of them in the kitchen. I blinked rapidly to stop myself from crying.

"How did you escape?"

I inhaled deeply. "The Ares let me go. King Memign told me they were programmed to do that to people who were their mother candidates."

We sat in silence sharing each other's pain and it was comforting.

"What's Christmas?" Cade suddenly asked and I laughed before diving into the details of what was once my favourite holiday.

CHAPTER NINETEEN

"We'll be there in less than an hour," Cade finally said.

After six hours cramped in the ship, it felt good to finally be getting ready. Cade handed me a long dagger and I recognized it immediately; it was definitely a two-horn's claw.

"It won't kill the upperclassmen, but it can still inflict damage. If you use it right."

I plucked it from his hand and slipped it into Sage's usual resting place.

Cade looked me up and down and I felt my face warm. He was too close but when I stepped away my back met wall.

"Why do you have so many holsters? Jut how many weapons are we rescuing?"

"Seven," I slowly said.

Cade's eyebrows shot upward. "*Seven?*" he said incredulously.

I suddenly felt like I couldn't look in his chocolatey brown eyes. What was wrong with me? This man was an alien! *Alien!* I repeated.

"Why so many?"

I shrugged. "It wasn't on purpose. I-I don't know!" I shoved him away from me. "Let's just get ready, okay?"

"Why are you so flustered?"

I rubbed my temples needing air. "I'm just anxious, alright? If I get caught... It's over."

Cade sobered. "For everyone. How is your knee?"

"Much better, thank you. I think running will be a strain but I have no choice."

In sombre silence, we watched as our ship approached Trireme. It loomed over us in all its glory. Turrets and towers sprung from the base of the ship. The Ares empire was indeed impressive. The ship likened a massive city. Overhead, a shipping dock was busy with activity.

"How do we get in?" I asked. "Won't they know it's an Almourrian ship?"

Cade nodded concentrating on where to fly the ship. He pointed to a dark spot hidden by rock and metal. "There." It was just big enough to dock our ship and close enough that slipping through the cracks in the rock would bring us straight on board. The ship powered down as Cade turned to me. "You ready?"

I nodded unable to speak.

Exiting the craft, we slipped through the shadowy rocks and came to a door. It opened once we got close but before entering, we peered around the corners. The hallway was empty.

Cade nodded. "Follow me."

We ran down a flight of stone steps to a long corridor with wooden doors. I was reminded of the dungeons but these doors were different and a loud noise emanated from within.

"What are behind these doors?" I asked cautiously.

"If I'm not mistaken, we should be able to find an engine bay. The door will be warm and beyond it is loud because the engines should be running. Each engine bay has a layout of the ship."

"Right."

Cade paused listening. Simultaneously we heard someone coming down the steps. Cade grabbed me and shoved me into the nearest door. It stunk of piss, blood, and sweat and was too dark to see what the room held. Pressing our ears against the door, we could hear someone thump heavily as they walked by and open a door across the hall. The door slammed shut behind them.

"Okay...I think we're good to go." I whispered.

Cade nodded. "I think so too. You smell nice."

"Ugh, focus!"

He chuckled and, after slowly opening the door, we ran along the corridor feeling the wooden boards and listening.

"I think I got it," Cade called in hushed tones.

We slipped inside keeping to the shadows. Huge nine-foot Ares, covered in soot and grime, lumbered about. Massive furnaces lined the walls and a clunking sound, like a metal heartbeat, sounded down below. The urge to peek over the railing that circled the center of the room was overwhelming but Cade grabbed my arm and pointed. The map was next to the furnaces with two metal beams acting as coverage. The problem was the well-lit open space between us and it. Returning would be just as difficult.

When we were sure no Ares were close, we silently ran to the beams but as we rounded the corner I inhaled sharply. An Ares was studying the map, a hand on his chin. In between the beams was a small place for us to hide. Cade covered the entrance with me inside and put his head down on my shoulder. We could not get caught. I held my breath as the Ares stomped by. Cade found my hand and squeezed it for support. Nodding, we both ran to the map.

"There," Cade said.

I could barely hear him above the ship's clunking and was therefore unconcerned about the Ares overhearing us. The room I was looking for was labelled "King's Vault".

"The king keeps all his especially valuable items in there," Cade explained.

"Wait. What if it's not there? Where else should I look?"

He looked doubtful but humoured me anyway. "Science and Research. It would make sense if you are going to mother the next generation that they would hold them in there."

Quickly finding it on the layout I mapped the directions in my head from the King's Vault and back to our ship. Returning to our dark corner was quick and easy. I was relatively certain we went unseen.

"Did you find the throne room?" I asked breathlessly.

Cade didn't respond but crept out the door and up the stairs so I was left with no choice but to follow him as I was going that way anyway.

"We need to find another staircase leading down."

The hallways remained empty but this place was huge, how was I ever going to find the right set of stairs? And Cade continued to follow me. I pulled him into an alcove with a large statue of the king, we were well hidden.

"What are you doing?" I hissed. "You need to find the throne room. Or his bed chambers. It's the middle of the night for them."

Cade grabbed my shoulders. "Silly woman, I'm coming with you."

I frowned. "But you said-"

He cut me off. "No, *you* said. Now come on. We need to find your things before they wake up."

The corridor went in a huge loop and about two thirds of the way in we spotted a staircase guarded by two soldiers, bigger than even the engine bay Ares. Their massive spears were the size of tree trunks.

"Our best chance is to come in from above."

"And how do you propose we do that?"

In awe I watched Cade nimbly climb a stone pillar and once he neared the ceiling, hop from one pillar to the next with ease until he was dangling above the guards. Neither one noticed a thing but my heart still raced anxiously and it nearly stopped as he dropped from above hanging only by his knees. With two-horn claw daggers in each hand he stabbed one in the base of the neck and while the second guard reacted to his comrade falling, Cade pounced stabbing the second guard in the chest. He staggered to his knee and Cade used the Ares's own spear to stab him through the gut. The guards were finished.

"Jane!" he whispered. "Help me!"

I realized I was standing there gawking in amazement. "Right," I mumbled.

It was like rolling two trees down the stairs. Removing the spears made the stairway look perfectly normal; hopefully it would buy us some time.

"I thought you said the claw daggers couldn't kill?"

"Did I? Huh."

It would appear Cade didn't want me to attempt fighting the Ares. True, I couldn't do any acrobatic stunts but I knew my way around daggers. Was this his way of protecting me?

Together we descended the dimly lit stairs and at the bottom was a big gold door with ornate fashioning's. It reminded me of the door leading to King Memign's courtroom; we were definitely on the right track.

When I tried the door, it merely jiggled.

"It's locked!" I hissed, panic setting in. Would we have time to find the key? Likely not, as I had no idea where to even begin looking.

Cade grabbed my shoulders and gave me a kind smile. "Want to see a special trick?" Taking the dagger, he sliced off one of the dead guards' hands and pressed it on the door handle. A click sounded from within and the door slid inward silently. Grabbing a torch from the wall, I led Cade inside, a blade at the ready just in case more guards lay in wait.

"Fingerprint reading?" I murmured. I never would have guessed that in this stone filled, torchlit corridor, such technology had been installed.

The room was enormous with gold, silver, and jewels of every kind lining its shelves and cluttering the floor.

"How are we supposed to find it in time?" I asked, daunted at the task ahead.

Cade surveyed the room in one quick sweep. "Given your weapons were most likely the newest objects in here I would say..." The word hung in the air as he traced their hiding place. "There."

A shelf on the far wall was only half filled with trinkets and on the bottom shelf, my weapons lay neatly piled. Dumped here because they were valuable only to soon be forgotten. Gathering my weapons, I placed them in their appropriate homes. Just as I was about to return Cade's dagger, I caught him looking me up and down again.

"Something you want to say?" I asked, an eyebrow uplifted.

Cade met my eyes. "No."

Taking the torch from me, we ran stealthily up the stairs but shouts could be heard from above. The missing guards had evidently been noticed. Both of us sprang into action stopping just before the entrance in order to gauge our opponents.

"Two," he mouthed to me and I nodded my understanding as I pulled out my axe. The metallic ring of metal on metal was unmistakable and an Ares drew near.

"Did you hear that?" a man asked.

Cade tucked and rolled, slicing the man's shins as he went before lunging at the next Ares, a tall woman in uniform. As the man stumbled forward, I sliced his neck with a lethal blow and focused my attention on Cade's attacker. She swung her spear expertly, trying to pin Cade down or knock him out, clearly wanting to keep him alive. Cade dodged and ducked with speed but kept getting in my way of a clean shot. I didn't want him to get in the cross fire of my axe so I opted for Gideon and Thomas. One stuck in her eye, the other her neck. There was a moment where she clawed to remove them but her mouth spurted black liquid and her cold yellow eyes glazed over in death.

Removing my blades, I wiped them on her shirt before Cade and I retraced our steps to *The Exagora*. But just as we rounded the bend in the loop, five Ares stood in our way chatting amiably. Once they saw us, swords were drawn and spears thrust ferociously in our direction. Cade prepared to lunge but I wrenched his arm back. Trusting me, he hung back and I swung my axe in large arcs. Golden light struck, slicing their chests twice. Black liquid burst forth and each one fell in a heap. The Ares who'd hung back survived and right as he began to yell out, Cade thrust his blades just above the collarbones and the man slumped over.

I stared at the wounds. If King Memign didn't recognize these, Queen Jezebel would.

"Cade, wait. If they recognize it's me, I'll put all of Almourr in danger. They'll know you helped me. We should stash the bodies." A thumping came from above, more guards no doubt.

"There isn't any time!" The synchronized thumping grew louder. "Come on!"

He grabbed my free hand and we ran for the shipping yard while trying to stay hidden. Ares' were everywhere now. We were running out of time.

CHAPTER TWENTY

Ducking behind the same statue as before, we waited until the marching soldiers passed on. Apparently, we were close to the barracks. When silence met our ears, we peered around the hands of the stone. As more time passed, more Ares filled the halls. Escape was becoming more difficult.

"What if we wait behind here until nightfall?" asked Cade.

"And lose a whole day? No. There isn't any time. Besides, once those guards are found, Trireme will be on high alert."

And that would be soon; the group that just passed us would happen upon them in mere moments. Taking our chance, we vaulted from our hiding place and ran for the exit. Barely escaping unseen, we leapt through the door blindly hoping the yard would be empty. But it was not to be. Ares of all sizes trudged by with loads over their shoulders and weapons at their hips. Many reacted immediately with swords and guns drawn. Swinging my axe cut down four or five allowing us a path towards *The Exagora* but more and more kept coming. This wouldn't be the clean exit we hoped for.

"Hurry to the ship!" I called. "I'll cover you."

Cade ran and I swung my axe. Black blood spurted everywhere covering everything in its vile filth including myself. He reached the cracks first and slipped through. With my back to the stone I swung one last arc and a brilliant gold light swept forth decimating nearly all the Ares within ten feet of me and injuring anyone else who managed to touch it. Not wasting a moment, I slipped in behind Cade. The rocks were too small for Ares to get though but who knew what else they could be capable of. As I stumbled through the cracks, Cade got *The Exagora* running and ready to flee. Scrambling aboard I urged him to fly but we had already exited our darkened alcove.

Breathlessly I slumped into the co-pilot's seat and shut my eyes. A smile crept over my face. We had done it.

Somewhere along the way I'd drifted to sleep and when I opened my eyes, I felt sore but well rested.

Cade was slumped comfortably in his chair gazing into the black abyss of space, his thoughts elsewhere. My movement caught his eye and he smiled at me.

Glancing at our attire I realized we were a mess. Blood crusted our arms and clothes, mine more so.

"Where did you learn to fight like that?" he asked as he stretched.

"Earth." I said stifling a yawn.

He smirked and unbuckled his seatbelt. "Earth is a two day's ride. Better get comfortable."

"Two days? In here? With you?" I croaked.

It would feel like an eternity. I'd known Cade for all of three days and half the time I was drooling over his sexy face while wanting to rip his head from his body the rest of the time. I couldn't handle the emotional rollercoaster. I would go insane.

Cade laughed self-consciously. "No need to worry. It won't be *that* bad."

It suddenly hit me. "You didn't kill the king."

"Nope."

I paused. "It was never your intention, was it?"

"Well, not really. If you wanted to kill him, great, but my real motive is to take down the entire race."

I threw my hands up in the air. "But you didn't even do that! You only succeeded in stealing my weapons back! I only want to save Earth. Why did you change your mind?"

Cade shrugged. "You can be really convincing."

Convincing? The whole time we'd talked I told him we'd go solo. Stunned to silence I stared at him, confused beyond belief. I finally found my voice. "What are you talking about?"

Cade stood up and fixed us each a glass of cool water I hadn't realized I was so parched until I accepted the drink. "I figure we have the same goals in the end. Once we save Earth, we can take down Trireme."

"*We?*" I asked, unable to keep the incredulousness from my voice.

He smiled that tempting smile, the one with the dimple. "Yes, we. The way I see it, I helped you, and now, you have to help me."

"No no no no! I could have done it myself!" Even to me that sounded like a lie and the man didn't miss a beat.

"Listen, Jane, I got you a ship to get you on Trireme and then killed those Ares standing guard. Face the facts, until you had your weapons you were basically useless. You needed me."

Flustered I began to protest. "No. I could've-"

"Nope. If they had captured you in a week's time, Earth would be destroyed and you would be in custody. Picked apart by some four-armed scientist."

I hated to admit it but he was right. Again. "You know, women don't like to be interrupted."

"Oh, my deepest apologies," he mockingly said.

I rolled my eyes.

Suddenly he became serious. "Thank you, by the way, for covering me back there."

"Twice," I gloated, still not fully able to be sincere. "And you're welcome."

Cade hid a smile as he plotted our course. Earth was so far away and the size of the universe had me gawking.

Silence reigned in the cabin once more. It was unbearable. Usually I was like Samuel, content to be quiet and observe. But since meeting Cade, I felt different. Like the me of my past, before the Ares, the one who loved to joke with her siblings, was re-emerging. And silence was tortuous.

"Cade, once Earth is safe, I don't intend to leave."

If we were in a car, he'd have slammed the brakes. "But I need you."

All smiles and mischievous humour was gone. Cade was being perfectly serious and I couldn't help but squirm under his scrutiny.

"Your weapons alone will change the balance." Ah. There it was again. He wanted my weapons, not me. "If you could create a blast powerful enough you could rip right through Trireme." He was saying and I thought back to the arena.

"I've been thinking and I am almost certain my weapons are in link with my emotional state."

Cade frowned but that caught his attention. "Go on," he urged.

"Back in the arena, I was so upset at the death of my friend that I lost it and swung blindly out of sheer rage. Tunnel vision, seeing red, that sort of thing. When I woke up, I was in a jail cell and King Memign told me I had destroyed the place."

Cade sat back thinking. "Well, if we win perhaps it will motivate you enough to be able to kill them all."

I wanted to say it wasn't my problem but I'd be kidding myself. How could I turn a blind eye after everything I'd seen? "Fine. I'll help you once we save Earth. How safe will it truly be anyway if we don't stop the Ares?"

Cade smiled deeply and I wanted to melt. Needing a break from the stunning view of a man I retreated to the washroom.

The next two days did not fly by. My time was interspersed with talk of our mission, long oppressive silences, and bland meals that tasted like plastic.

"Cade," I finally said staring at the ceiling.

The day had been exhausting. Our chairs reclined down to become beds and we were turning in for the night.

"Yes, Jane."

I had to admit, I loved it when he used my full name, not that I'd given him another option.

"Tell me something."

He shifted on the cot to face me. "What?"

"Something interesting. About Almourr or your family. Or who you want to actually marry."

Cade leaned back and faced the ceiling as well. It was as good a view as any it seemed.

"Actually, I can't marry anyone now."

I whipped around to look at him. "What do you mean?"

Cade slowly turned to look at me. "Yeah. Almourrians don't divorce or re-marry like most places. Once you engage to marry someone you are pledged to that person until you die."

"What!? How could you just get engaged to me like that? Now you can't be with anyone. How could you?"

Cade smiled, a mischievous light in his eyes. "I couldn't resist your dazzling blue eyes and enchanting face."

I groaned loudly. "Jokes aside, why?"

Cade frowned and glanced at me, all serious. "Who says I'm joking?"

"Because I don't have blue eyes."

He sat up alarmed. "What?" Grabbing my arm, he pulled me up to check even though it was dark. "You do so."

I laughed and he smiled at my joke. "Seriously though, Cade. Why throw away your future like that? You won't have an heir or a wife. You'll be alone. Forever." A sadness I couldn't stop seeped into my voice. Once his father was gone, he'd have no one. I was alone now and it was terrible and didn't wish him the same fate.

"Three hundred years isn't that bad. And I could always adopt children. And to answer your question, I came on this mission to ensure the future of Almourr. And it's the right thing to do."

"I'm sorry, did you just say *three hundred* years?" I was too distracted by this to admire his heroics.

"Yes. That is the average age of my people."

Trying to digest that I asked another question. "How old are you then?"

"I'll be fifty-seven next month."

I leaned back on my cot and closed my eyes. My father had been sixty when he died. A fresh pool of unforeseen tears threatened to emerge. How silly. And we had been having so much fun.

I hadn't realized how long I'd remained silent.

"Is that so strange?" he suddenly asked.

"On Earth yes. We live to be maybe one hundred."

"Because you have a gaseous sun and we do not."

That made sense... Sort of. Our sun gave us wrinkles and cancer and all sorts of other things so it made sense, the shorter life span.

"Fascinating," I managed to say.

He spent the next hour regaling me of tales of his youth and home. Exhaustion crept into my voice but I was no less interested. Cade heard it and bid me goodnight.

"Tomorrow, we talk about Earth."

I scoffed. "Goodnight, Cade."

CHAPTER TWENTY-ONE

"You mean humans have never travelled to Gi? It's only one galaxy away!"

Cade was incredulous at Earth's apparent lack of sophistication.

"At least we have doors," I muttered.

He stretched. We'd be arriving in the Milky Way soon and it had me giddy. Truthfully, I hadn't been gone that long, hardly a week but it still felt like a lifetime. The day had been flying by. Cade and I seemed to be able to put our differences aside to actually enjoy each other's company. Who was I kidding? I'd liked him since day one.

"Wow, Earth isn't nearly as sexy as Almourr."

I spurted the tea I'd been drinking out of my mouth and was thrown into a coughing fit.

"What?" I said, trying my best not to laugh.

"Huge, right?" Cade looked confused and slightly embarrassed. "Did I use the word incorrectly?"

Biting back a laugh I shook my head. "No, no, you did! I just… The tea went down the wrong pipe."

"Oh. Are you alright then?"

Clearing my throat, I nodded vigorously then proceeded to drink again in order to hide my smile.

"I noticed that too, actually. Almourr is at least double the size of Earth," I commented.

Together we watched in awe as Earth slowly got bigger and bigger. The blue water remained and the green continents were intact, just as I'd left her. It was like a weight lifted from my shoulders. I hadn't realized I'd been so worried.

"Where will the bomb be?" I asked.

Cade snapped around to look at me. "You mean you don't know?"

"*You* don't know!?" I began pacing the small cabin. "We have maybe a day to find it! There is no way we can scour the whole planet!" I stopped. "Why are you smiling?"

Cade chuckled. "I just wanted to see you freak out. I know how we can find it."

I groaned angrily. "You!" I smacked him hard on the arm. "Now isn't the time for jokes!" Huffing angrily, I flung myself onto the seat.

Growing serious, he explained how the tracking system worked. "This machine was built into all our ships. It tracks Ares technology, analyzes it, and identifies its exact location and purpose."

As we came closer to the planet the system came online.

Allowing him to work in peace, I gazed at my home planet in amazement. It was truly beautiful. I'd never thought I'd get to see Earth from such an angle. The thought of space travel always terrified me and yet here I was.

The screen beeped and blinked red. "Got it." Cade announced. "Do you know where that is?"

I looked at the map. "Canada… Somewhere. Can you fly to that exact place?"

Cade glanced up at me. "Yes. But it will be heavily guarded by Ares troops, and not the little ones."

"Do you have more weapons than just those daggers?"

"Yes. In that hatch down there."

Pointing in the right direction, I followed his finger and began unloading his weapons. Two big guns and a broadsword, he should be set.

Even though I was buckled in tightly, I still clutched the chair in a deathly grip as we descended through Earth's atmosphere. It was a bumpy ride with us jerking about and for a minute we couldn't see anything but smoke and dust. My stomach lurched. I hated rollercoasters, they made me motion sick and this was all too similar. Cade was focused with his brows furrowed and his eyes locked on the screen. He didn't seem to notice my distress.

Once we broke through, the rumbling stopped and the flying smoothed out once more. I inhaled deeply, needing fresh air but settled at the wondrous sight of home.

"Are you alright?" asked Cade.

He shot me a quick glance, still focusing on the task at hand. Apparently flying in an environment that lacked gravity was different from one that didn't, still, my heart warmed at his concern.

"Fine. I'll be fine once we land," I assured him.

Canada was filled with monstrous mountains, never-ending fields, and flourishing forests. The place seemed an untouched oasis but I knew that if we encountered a town, the serene perspective would be shattered.

The Exagora hovered above a quiet clearing and Cade landed her softly in the luscious grass.

I wanted to scramble out of the stagnant cabin and breathe fresh air but knew Ares were lurking about so opted for a cool glass of water instead.

Cade geared up and I followed suit. Once we were battle ready, Cade unfolded a plan.

"I've dealt with these planet destroyer bombs before. They are implanted into the ground on the first wave of attack. Like a plant, it has root-like veins that burrow into the ground until it reaches the core of the planet."

I rubbed my chin in thought. "So, if it explodes it reaches the core? Thus, destroying the whole planet?"

"Exactly," he confirmed. "There will be a red light; once it starts blinking, you're too late, the bomb will be armed and it will be all over." He let that sink in before continuing. "So, we need to dismantle the bomb before removing the roots." Anticipating my next question, he explained further. "If you try removing the roots first, the bomb will activate and blow up. Removing the roots is no easy task. I will disarm the bomb, you cover us with your axe, deal?"

"Seems easy enough," I replied.

The door hissed as it opened and we slipped outside. After carefully surveying the surrounding landscape, we ran up the hill. The bomb was in a clearing beyond the ridge. We lay on our stomachs taking it all in. Sure enough, day crawlers swarmed the area and no doubt night guards lay slumbering in wait. We were in luck, it was early morning and the sun had only risen hours before, night guards wouldn't be an issue.

With every stomp of a day crawler, the ground shook and seeing the bomb's location seemed more and more impossible to reach. My patience was growing thin and I poked Cade. "Why don't we just go in there, gun's blazing?"

He frowned. "You don't have any guns."

"It's an expression!" I whispered angrily but seeing his face I knew he was teasing. Rolling my eyes, I unsheathed my axe.

"You don't want to wait?" he pressed.

"My mom always used to say there's no time like the present."

Cade crinkled his nose. "Really?"

"No."

Swinging my axe as hard as I could I flung myself into the fray. Cade shot past me ducking out of the way of swinging day crawlers and using dead ones as launch pads to jump above the rest. The man was certainly nimble but I couldn't let him distract me.

Golden arcs shot upwards killing two at once and incidentally their twin counterparts. The ground rumbled as they fell. I ran forward trying to keep up with Cade. The ground was damp in the early morning. Cade had already run out of bullets and was expertly thrusting his sword, injuring Ares just enough to move past them. It made my job of killing the wounded aliens much easier.

The light cut through the Ares with ease and I had to jump out of the way of falling day crawlers.

The corpses of the day crawlers acted as a wall even I had trouble getting over what with poison leaking from their eyes and the slippery bloodied bodies. But it proved to be an ally buying us time. The massive day crawlers also struggled and most failed to get over them. If they did reach the top, I purposefully delivered a lethal blow, adding height to our wall.

"Make sure you cut us an exit," warned Cade gravely and I obeyed, making sure it was in the direction of our ship.

The bomb was in clear sight. As Cade and I grew near, a strange roar erupted from the trapped day crawlers.

"They're calling the others!" cried Cade.

We reached the bomb and Cade used his sword to pop off the sealed lid. The planet killer was a large box, the size of a desk. Wires and hoses were connected within and the bomb was embedded in the ground.

"Don't touch the roots," cautioned Cade.

I couldn't watch him work. Night guards emerged from within the woods. These ones looked different from usual. They had blue iridescent stripes down their backs and had six legs instead of four, but they still lacked eyes and their tails were still like whips.

Keeping the daggers sheathed, I swung my axe back and forth with momentum but they kept coming in droves. Fighting fatigue, I ordered my arms to continue.

"You can do this, Jane." I whispered.

Behind me, Cade grunted, doing his best to be careful and work quickly.

Corpses lay strewn all over the field, mangled and bleeding. The stench of it overwhelmed my senses but I still pushed on.

I unsheathed Thomas and in one hand I was slicing with it while the other the axe burst forth golden arcs, decimating all within a ten-foot radius.

Calmly I waited for the next horde to surface over the wall of corpses. In the distance I could hear them snarling and the ground shaking as they ran.

"Hurry! Before a horde forms!" I yelled.

I was losing strength. I glanced at Cade and was certain he didn't quite know what he was doing. His hands slid carefully over and under the compartments but he hesitated and didn't pull out any wires. Luckily the red light still shone brilliantly. We still had time. It could shine for the next two days for all we knew.

The ground rumbled in the distance and grew louder. Night guards charged full speed towards us. Their mouths dripped with saliva and their claws were caked with the blood of fallen comrades. Tightening my grip on my weapons, I raised my axe above my head, waiting for the right moment to strike. Once the closely-knit group of Ares was within ten feet of me, I could slash the aliens and decimate them all in one stroke.

"Jane…" Cade's voice was tight with dread but I couldn't lose focus.

Just as I was about to drop my arm something passed through me, like a cold shiver, and all the night guards dropped, skidding to a stop. I had to run out of the way to stop from being trampled. I nearly tripped in the damp grass. At first, I thought them dead but upon closer inspection I found their eyes were closed but they were breathing; only asleep.

"Jane!"

"What?" I snapped, running towards him.

A dead two-horn lay at his feet. "It touched this panel before I could kill it. I don't know what happened." Cade explained. A strange antenna had lifted from within the bomb. "It let out some sort of signal. You felt it right?" I thought of the cold shiver that ran through me. "It must have put them to sleep." He gestured to the horde.

Looking around the clearing, it seemed all the Ares' were asleep. There was no more grunting and the ground no longer rumbled. The familiar feeling of dread rose up inside me.

I didn't like this. "Cade, what's going on?"

"Jane." Cade's voice was tense. "We have to go. Look." The red light was blinking. Before I could protest, Cade grabbed me and began running toward the ship.

Freeing myself from his grasp I hung back. "No!" Quickly I sheathed my axe. "We have to defuse it somehow."

Cade rubbed a hand anxiously through his hair. "You don't understand. Once the light blinks there *is* no way to defuse it."

I fought tears. "You don't know that. I… I have to try." Cade came close cautiously. "You go back to the ship. Get away while you still can."

He folded his arms and that devilish grin crossed his face. "Well that won't do."

I smiled in relief. He'd stay to help me.

Returning as quickly as we could we tried to see the bomb with new eyes.

"Maybe if I just slice it with my axe?"

"No! Don't you know how bombs work?"

"Well at least I'm offering ideas!"

Cade bit back a retort. "Let's focus. We don't have much time."

I couldn't even begin to decipher what it all meant. There were no coloured wires and most of them went deeper into the bomb. I couldn't face the cold truth. Was there truly nothing we could do? My breathing grew short and I grew light-headed. I had to do *something*.

Without thinking I ripped out the largest metal hose. A strange greenish vapour drifted out of the hose. The red light began blinking faster.

"Now we really have to go. Jane."

I couldn't suppress the sobs. "Cade. I can't. Maybe…" I looked at the blinking light, a countdown to our doom. "If I just…"

Cade grabbed me by the waist and swung me over his shoulder. Sprinting for the exit even as I kicked and screamed irrationally wanting to stay. I couldn't leave them. If there was any chance even one person was out there, I had to try! Tears streamed down my face and sobs racked my body. Freeing myself of his grasp once more I tried to run back.

"Sorry, Jane."

I didn't see his fist coming. When I opened my eyes, the world was upside down, my head hurt, and the dizziness made comprehending my surroundings impossible. Cade had me dangled over his shoulder running toward *The*

Exagora. The ground was shaking and up ahead the mountains were crumbling. Trying to fight him proved impossible as I had no strength.

Once in the ship, Cade strapped me in my chair before punching in coordinates with newfound speed. After buckling himself in the ship took off and began its ascent into the heavens.

Tears streamed down my face. In a daze I watched as fire engulfed the trees below and once we reached space, I could see it was everywhere. The planet glowed like the sun. The bomb had gone off; even from space we could see the mushroom cloud. The planet was ripped open like a wound, its inner workings lay bare and bleeding. The fire was consuming the planet with frightening speed. Cade let the ship hover from a safe distance and I couldn't make a sound, unable to move I watched my home be destroyed. Like a waterfall, the tears fell unceasingly.

"I don't want to see anymore." I whispered. Closing my eyes, I felt the ship turn and dart away from the horrific scene.

CHAPTER TWENTY-TWO

Cade handed me a glass of water and a dish of what I assumed was Almourrian food. Without thinking I drank and ate. Finding a blanket, he draped it over my shoulders and sat across from me with tortured eyes.

Everyone was gone, I knew it with certainty now. It hadn't occurred to me how much faith I had riding on the hope that my friends were alive. It was a silly notion, really. The chances that anyone had survived the massacre at the safe camp was negligible.

Seeing Harriet's smiling face in my mind's eye and the thought of the baby growing inside her brought fresh tears. Swiping them away I sniffed and looked up at Cade.

"I'm so sorry, Jane. I... couldn't lose anyone else." His voice was barely above a whisper.

I wanted to smile but my face wouldn't cooperate. "It's alright Cade. You did the right thing. I was acting irrationally."

"My brother died from an Ares bomb." Understanding grew between us. "We were lucky, the Ares detonated it in a last-ditch effort to annihilate us but the roots hadn't reached the planet's core. That's the real reason it's mainly a desert now."

Exhaustion swept over me and my head hurt from crying so much. Sipping on the water helped but all I wanted was to crawl into a dark hole and sleep.

"You should sleep. I set a course to return to Almourr."

Changing my seat into a cot I turned over to sleep but it wouldn't come. What would I do now? There was nothing left. Nothing. I slept long and hard but when I awoke felt like I hadn't slept a wink. Stretching, I sat up and found Cade shirtless in front of the sink and mirror cleaning a wound.

"You're hurt!" I croaked leaping from my cot. But the room did a spin and I stumbled. Cade caught me and gently set me on my feet.

I squinted at him suspiciously. "Did you put something in my water?" Cade said nothing. "You *did*, didn't you!"

"It was just to help you sleep," he sheepishly said.

"You can't keep doing that!" I looked upward praying for strength and. reminding myself he was hurt, I chose to look past it. Ordering him into the chair, I found clean dressings and a bottle labelled *sanitation liquid*. Hoping it would burn, I plucked it from the shelf.

"How long was I out?" I asked taking a seat across form him.

"About a day."

Ignoring his smouldering stare, I leaned in to inspect the wound. "What happened?"

Shifting uncomfortably in his chair, he cleared his throat. "An Ares whipped me in its sleep while I was running to the ship."

"That would explain my aching shoulder." I dipped the cloth into the liquid and dabbed it on the wound. He grunted in pain and I bit my lip before applying the inner band aid.

"Why are you holding your breath?"

I looked up into his warm chocolatey eyes and stuttered. It was all very overwhelming. His eyes, warmth, and scent were all too much and to top it off I felt my face warm. "I don't want to hurt you." I confessed.

He smiled. "You won't."

We didn't have any tape which meant I had to wrap the gauze around his torso and pin it. I suddenly regretted that I had insisted on helping. My hands were cold and I had to hug him closely in order to get around his waist. The silence shrouding us was heavy but not uncomfortable. Cade's breathing was deep and even. Finally, I pinned the gauze in place and stepped back. He rubbed his eyes and threw on a fresh shirt.

"Have you slept at all?"

He grinned. "No."

I began dismantling his chair into a cot. "You need to go to sleep."

"That's so sweet. You're worried about me." A mischievous glint lit his eyes.

"Actually, I don't know how to fly the ship, so..." I pointed to the cot, he slipped onto it and I laid my blanket on top of him. It wasn't long before his breathing became deep and his eyes were closed. I gawked freely. How could a man be so handsome and chiseled and funny and caring? I easily forgot he was an alien, he looked human after all. He made me forget my past troubles. Nightmares about

Luke or my family had ceased since meeting him. In that moment I realized why: Cade made me feel safe.

Growing self-conscious with my revelation, I moved to the sink. The ship was small and lacked a proper washroom, and I settled in front of the mirror with a cloth to clean my arms and face. Peeling off the stinky shirt, I inspected the damage. A massive pink and purple bruise radiated across my shoulder. Evidently, I'd hit a rock in our little tumble. Small bruises and cuts covered my legs but the cuts on my back and arm were healing nicely. In the cupboard, I found backup clothes. The pants fit and it felt nice to put on fresh clothes. I could only find an oversized seater, probably Cade's, but slipped it on anyway. My face had a swollen, darkening green bruise on my cheek where Cade had punched me. Poor man probably felt bad every time he looked at it. I became resolved to thank him. If it weren't for him, I would have died in the bomb blast along with every other human.

How many people had suffered the same fate as us? The Ares had to be stopped.

Splashing water in my face once more, I continued the tedious task of cleaning the dirt out from underneath my fingernails. Lifting my bruised shoulder proved painful and nearly impossible, but I managed to pull my hair back into a thick French braid and glared at my reflection critically. I always liked the way I looked, but could a man like Cade ever like me back?

I groaned into the cloth. Here I was contemplating where a man's affections lay when our next step was war. Still, the distraction was easier than thoughts of Earth. Just the name brought an onslaught of more tears. I sat on the bench by the sink and let the tears fall. Stifling sobs to let Cade sleep, I cried for several hours. I felt so lost and alone in the dark. Gazing out the small oval window, I imagined Earth light years away, burning. Disintegrating into nothing. Like it was never there. I could see the moon tilting off its orbit, spinning away into another planet. More destruction. Would it ever end?

My head spun in circles and my eyes burned. I had never cried so hard in my life. Using the sweater to swipe tears away had long since proven pointless as more and more tears fell. My head felt so heavy and just when I thought I'd nothing left to give, Cade was there encircling me in his arms. I clung to his shirt and sobbed. Usually I detested crying in the presence of others but now I didn't care. He rubbed my back slowly, being careful of my wounds.

Neither of us needed words. It was comforting enough to sit like that in a starlit night.

Eventually the tears stopped and I calmed down enough to feel self-conscious again. But when I went to pull away Cade locked his arms. "Don't move."

Truthfully, I didn't want to. He was so warm and his embrace so comforting. I closed my eyes.

"Thank you for everything," I mumbled into his shoulder.

He laid his head on mine. "You're welcome."

I could feel myself relax and my senses fade away as sleep overtook me. At the back of my mind I remembered where I was and jolting myself awake, I sprang from his arms. Cade looked like he'd also been asleep and I caught a glimpse of myself in the mirror. I, too, looked terrible.

My eyes were puffy and bloodshot and my bruised cheek looked worse than before.

"I... I need to go to sleep." Even forming words seemed difficult. "But you too, though."

Cade looked at me as a parent might a child, a curious smile lifted the corners of his mouth. Was he disappointed? I was so exhausted I couldn't think. I stumbled to the cot and crawled onto it. My head hit the pillow and I was out.

When I finally stirred, I knew it had been a long time even though the scenery remained the same – stars, stars, and more endless stars. A blanket had been placed over me and my shoes had been removed. My body felt stiff from lack of movement but when I went to stretch, my shoulder protested. My first thought was for water, so I creeped out of bed and poured myself a glass.

Autopilot said Almourr was two hours away. I was actually glad to be returning but then a thought hit me and I nearly dropped my cup. Cade and I were engaged. To be married.

CHAPTER TWENTY-THREE

King Edgarr was at the shipping yard, angrily awaiting our arrival. His embroidered robes fluttered in the wind, decidedly complementing the king's outrage. Brigham accompanied him.

"What's going to happen?" I asked timidly as we approached.

Cade's smile was unconcerned as he waved at his father. "He'll probably force us to get married this week and ground me to the planet for a century. No biggie."

"But we aren't actually engaged. Can't you just explain?"

Cade put his hand around my waist and I gasped. "By all laws on Almourr we are. Marriage is very sacred here."

And then we were meeting face to face. The king reigned in his anger when he looked at me but the daggers he sent towards Cade sent chills down even my spine.

"Cade, Miss Jane. A word." His tone brooked no argument and so we helplessly followed him.

Once in private quarters, King Edgarr let loose. His calm demeanor was a complete façade. The king was toe to toe with Cade, so close, in fact, I could see spit flying but Cade took it with grace. "How could you take your betrothed *alone* for almost *five* days in a small ship?" He wrung his hands in anger. I almost wondered if he did it so he wouldn't wring Cade's neck. "You are Almourr's first prince! The future king! How could you be so reckless? I understand what it's like to be young and impatient, but still, Brigham was a perfectly capable chaperone." I cringed at impatient. "He can take care of himself in a fight and is a friendly sort of fellow. Who wouldn't want him along?" The bruise on his face matched mine and I swallowed a giggle.

Brigham began to reiterate but the king told him to shut it. "You are only here because you witnessed the event!"

Cade took this moment to intervene. "How many people know?"

The king exhaled, visibly relaxing. "No one, thanks to Brigham here. He hid in a closet until the yard was deserted and came straight to me." Cade and I shared a glance before locking eyes with Brigham. He turned crimson and looked away in shame.

"Now. Here is what is going to happen. Miss Jane will live under your roof as is custom but *with* Brigham to chaperone you and in two week's time, you shall be wed at the midnight Beacon, understood?"

Cade smiled and pulled me close. "We wouldn't have it any other way."

"There is a ball tonight where we shall publicly announce the betrothal. Be prepared, please." We bowed and exited. I was too dazed to even comment but Cade was beaming.

"That went better than expected! We have to get you clothes and an earring. And how to convince my father of letting us leave again?"

I realized he was no longer talking with me so I followed in silent anger. Once we reached his home I cut into his incoherent babbling.

"Cade!"

He turned, eyes wide, all innocence.

"This was all fine until," I swallowed hard, "Earth was destroyed. Now we *actually* have to get married?"

Cade absorbed that. "I am sorry. Truly. But it's out of my hands. How about we deal with that when we get to it? There are some important things I need to tend to."

My anger flared. "Like what?"

He stepped close and observed my ear, caressing it ever so gently. "Your ears are pierced, right?"

Shivers ran down my spine.

A man cleared his throat and stepped out of the shadows, revealing it to be Brigham. "Prince Cade, I trust you will keep a practical distance from Miss Jane?"

Cade dropped his hand but he didn't seem the least bit put out. "Come, Brigham! We have much to do!"

Both men left me standing in the entryway. It was all so overwhelming. It had never occurred to me that I'd be returning here. The planet was exquisite but could it ever really be home? I had joked of retiring here but now that it wasn't a choice it seemed less enticing.

After bathing in the creek, I sat on a stool bundled up in a housecoat as Everest did my hair and makeup. "Your skin is so pale! And no markings! How unique." Her own arms were covered in the same black bands and by her tone I could tell she wasn't insulting me; she was genuinely intrigued.

A knock sounded from the hall and Cade ducked in, package in hand. Everest immediately bowed and exited.

"Your dress, milady." I opened the box and lifted out a deep purple dress. It went to the floor and tied around my neck in an adorable little bow. The back was completely open and the fabric swayed daintily in the constant slight breeze.

"It's lovely," I gasped.

Cade looked pleased but frowned when my own brows furrowed. "What the matter?"

"I bruised my shoulder. It's quite ghastly. Do you think it will look bad?" I turned around and exposed my bare shoulder, revealing the intense bruise. I turned at his gasp, feeling even more self-conscious than before but it was in fact Brigham who'd walked in rather untimely. His face was beet red.

"My lady! You cannot undress in front of his highness until after the wedding!"

He couldn't meet my eye as he ushered Cade from the room. I could hear him berating my fiancé for entering my chambers without him. Chuckling, I began putting on the dress. The straps pressed on my bruise uncomfortably and the black and purple discolouration covering my shoulder was in plain view. Besides that, the dress was captivating. How did he come up with this stuff? Just as I was about to slip on the matching sandals a knock sounded at my hallway again. Cade peeked inside as if he weren't supposed to be there.

I folded my arms. "Yes?"

He appraised me up and down. "You look incredible."

There was a 'but' in there somewhere. He went behind me fingering my shoulder. I winced at the pressure.

"Jane, Again, I am so-"

I cut him off. "No need, Cade. You've saved me twice now. There no need for more apologies." I touched his arm in reassurance.

His apologetic look was masked by his excitement at presenting yet another box.

"This dress is fine," I insisted.

"No, no. We'll be dancing all night and you should be comfortable." He pushed the box at me and I took it from him.

"Where did you get this on such short notice? Do you just have dresses in my size for every occasion?" I joked.

"Yes. There is a whole room full. Now open it. Before Brigham gets back."

I honestly couldn't tell if he was joking or not but obliged and lifted the lid off slowly. The dress beneath was gorgeous. It was white with yellow beading and embroidery. Diamonds made the bust glisten in the starlight. My breath caught. The floor length dress was fitted with a corset that had yellow strings. I could adjust the size to allow for breathing room for my bruise and wound. The dress had capped sleeves and a keyhole in front which meant the bruise was completely hidden. It flared out at the waist in silky folds. I loved it.

"My lady? Is Prince Cade with you?"

Our eyes widened as Brigham's voice grew dangerously close. Without warning, Cade leapt out the window and ran around the house.

"No." I said honestly. "Perhaps check outside?"

He thanked me and left. Everest returned to help cinch me up and finished with yellow and white gems in my hair.

"You look amazing," said Everest, a touch of envy in her voice.

"Do men always dress their wives here?"

"Oh yes. In the past it was customary and unthinkable for a woman to shop for herself but now it is more for large events that they order a dress for you. Not to wear it is insulting."

I stared at the purple dress discarded on the bed. "Did I just insult the prince?"

Everest glanced at it as well. "I don't think so. He was so excited to go get this one for you. I overheard him muttering how it was much more suitable than the purple one."

"Do I at least get to pick out my wedding dress?" I asked bleakly.

"Of course! It is the one occasion where you dress for him, in order to please him. Wedding dresses are a huge deal here."

I smiled, happy we could relate about something. "Me too. At home it was a billion-dollar business."

Everest looked puzzled. "Billion? I don't know that word."

I hesitated thinking of how to explain. "It was a big also a big deal at home. A lot of money involved."

She smiled, satisfied with the explanation.

"Everest. At home it was customary to take your mother, sisters, and friends to go wedding dress shopping.

You are my only friend here; might you accompany me?" I held my breath worrying I might have stepped over some sort of boundary.

But my fear was misplaced. She threw the perfume bottle into the air and grabbed me into a fierce hug. "Oh, I'd love to! Nothing could be grander!"

I gasped for breath and gained my senses as she ran from the room giddy with excitement. My back was throbbing but it was worth it.

I slipped into the lace shoes and made my way to the entrance. Cade looked amazing in a black suit. Upon closer inspection it was different from what I was used to, but he was clean cut and his bulging muscles still showed. He held a small black box in his hands. Slowly, he looked me up and down and I blushed. "You look ravishing."

"You as well." I managed to say.

His smile deepened revealing those dimples and I felt ready to swoon. Marrying him wouldn't be that bad but I could never let him know that.

"Here. This is for you." He handed me the black box and I began opening it curiously.

"So many boxes in one day." I saw Brigham just outside, tapping his foot impatiently. "My but chaperones are in a hurry," I commented, loud enough for him to hear.

When he saw me, his jaw dropped and he stopped moving altogether. My face warmed under the attention.

Cade pulled me close and whispered in my ear. "You human girls are insatiable flirts."

I swatted him away needing to cool down but when I saw the contents of the box I gasped. A diamond stud and a golden teardrop earring lay inside. The gold was etched with designs of flowers and leaves with tiny diamonds dotting the buds. A refusal was on my lips when he cut in. "It's a sign of our engagement. Everyone expects it." I slipped them on and showed them off for his amusement.

"Lovely."

I took the elbow he held out to me and let him guide me toward the party. Brigham hung back in order to make sure nothing inappropriate occurred.

The Beacon's light was fading and the evening blooms began to glow, it was becoming my favourite part of the day. It was like living among the stars. On this planet they were so bright and you could see them so clearly.

Cade halted in front of the huge wooden ballroom doors. "Are you ready?"

Inhaling deeply to calm myself, I nodded. "I think so."

He'd told me that afternoon of his plans to win over the aristocracy. Basically, charm the socks off them until they couldn't help but agree. Thing was, I wasn't that charming.

CHAPTER TWENTY-FOUR

The room was spectacular. Branches hung high above with bright flowers blooming overhead and vines rippled around the supporting pillars offering more light. A band played soft music on instruments I'd never heard of and food was piled high on surrounding tables. Everyone was dressed so elegantly, there was no shortage of lace, embroidery, or silk.

King Edgarr quickly found us and herded us into the room like sheep. Then he began introducing me as his future daughter to a sea of faces I couldn't even begin to remember. Most people attending were nobility, the rest were politicians.

Cade whispered in my ear so I could hear above the hum of conversation. "You've met the most important men. As I suspected, you've dazzled them in that dress. Now you must charm them. I will deal with the highest-ranking officials. That group to your left should be an easy target. Remember, the goal is to get one of them to ask my father for a ship."

Pulling him aside, I planted my hands on my hips. "I've been thinking... We need to go bigger. Just the two of us is nearly impossible. But what if we took an envoy to the Eirene and got them to ally with us?"

"They would never do that."

"Why not? The enemy of my enemy is my friend, no?"

Cade rubbed his chin, clearly thinking it over. "Fine. But you cannot come."

My hands met my hips again and I had to stop from shouting. "What? I thought the Eirene were somewhat peaceful?"

"No, not the envoy, on the mission."

"*What*?!" I hissed. "Why not?"

"You are the Ares' most wanted. You can't waltz in there to kill the king. It's too dangerous."

"Listen here, *fiancé*, you owe me one, seeing as I have to be stuck married to you for the rest of my life!" Lifting my skirts, I stormed off to get a glass of punch.

Ladies adorned in too many sparkles and too-tight corsets surrounded the punch table. When they turned to glare at me, I thought their breasts would pop out of the dress and purposely averted my gaze so as not to stare.

"You, the little human girl, is marrying our dear Prince Cade?" one of them said, sniffing in disbelief. But upon spying my earring her face grew red and she frantically ran from the table. All the other ladies backed down as well. How interesting.

"Don't mind them." A tall graceful girl about my age glided up, two cups of punch in her hand. I noticed an earring similar to mine dangling from her ear marking her as married. "I am Tamika. How are you enjoying this evening?" she asked.

"Jane," I replied, smiling. "Truthfully? I have no idea what I'm doing. Plus, the prince and I need to speak with as many politicians as we can to ask a favour."

"A favour?" Her eyes gleamed. "Do go on."

I spilled the details about needing an envoy to entice the Eirenites to make an alliance.

Suddenly, she grabbed my arm and whisked me to a group of men all of varying ages.

"Dear, this is Miss Jane. She has something she'd like to ask you."

The evening went on in such a manner. Tamika was married to a judge in the highest court who was able to gain me easy access into the right groups. Convincing them of our plot was easy when the pain was still fresh in my mind.

Standing alone on the balcony inspecting glowing flowers gave me a nice break. The evening had been successful. Cade came trotting up, ruining my quiet moment.

"The king accepted! The day after tomorrow, we'll ride for Eirene with Brigham," I rolled my eyes, "and two politicians. I will act on behalf of the monarchy and you are the would-be mother! This is brilliant!"

He handed me a glass of bubbly liquid and clinked our glasses. I'd never seen him so happy but shared in it nonetheless. I was glad to know everything was going to smoothly.

"The Ares have come and gone to pick me up. How does that work?" I hadn't been able to stop thinking about it.

"They read your DNA and vital signs. Good thing you were off-planet when they scanned, otherwise, they would have found you."

I nodded, relieved that there was one less thing to worry about.

Silence settled between us as we watched the garden glowing in all its magnificence. Cade looked around and I followed his gaze. Brigham was busy chatting up a young woman and for once, wasn't staring at us.

Cade grabbed my hand, pulling me around the side of the house and out of sight. "Come on," he whispered and we fled from the garden.

My knee was feeling much better so keeping up this time wasn't so difficult.

"Cade, what's going on?" I asked, struggling not to step on any of the layers of fabric.

"I want to show you something."

Once we were a good distance from the ball, Cade slowed to a walk, still clutching my hand. Slowly, I withdrew it from his grasp. He didn't seem to notice and I felt disappointed. Cade was too busy chatting about tomorrow's plans and the mission at hand. I'd never seen him this animated. We drew near his home and I frowned.

"What was it you wanted to show me?"

He smiled in the dimly lit path. "It's a surprise."

Following Cade into the house, he led me through what seemed a maze of hallways and corridors before it opened up into a massive inner courtyard that was filled with the most amazing garden I'd ever seen. Impossible trees were planted near the entrance, their leaves hovering in place. When I went to touch one, the leaf drifted to the grass and promptly shrivelled into a brown crunchy heap upon impact.

Flowers consumed the garden. They were absolutely everywhere, entwining themselves around pillars and lining the pathways. A creek bubbled through the courtyard and disappeared into the house. I'd never been in this part of the house before and what a sight I'd missed! Every one of the plants looked unique, I hadn't seen them in the village at all.

"Every plant here is from another planet or is very rare. I've spent years collecting them. Before the Ares attacked it was a sort of hobby of mine, and my collection was much larger." He peered around to look at my face, evidently pleased with what he saw. "Do you like it?"

"It's…incredible." I was rendered speechless.

"Come. This isn't what I wanted to show you."

My brows knit together curiously. It wasn't?

Guiding me down the path, we crossed a low stone bridge leading us over the creek. Nestled at the foot of a short leafless red tree was a lone flower. It looked exactly like a daisy.

"Is that…?" I looked up at him and he beamed.

"It is! When we fell on Earth, this flower got caught in my boot. I was able to save it. Now it can grow here as a reminder of your home."

Tears burned at the back of my throat. It was the best surprise anyone had ever given me. I didn't know what to say. I went to bend down on my knees but Cade caught my arms.

"I want to look closer," I protested.

"Not in that dress. It'll get all dirty."

I glanced at the rich white fabric. He was right. I laughed thinking how ridiculous he was to be thinking about that right now.

"Thank you, Cade. This is amazing." I gave him a big hug catching him off guard.

His hands wrapped around me and we hugged for a long time. "It was my pleasure." He finally said.

"Ahem!"

An angry grunt sounded from behind us. We didn't have to look to know it was Brigham. His face was red and his chest heaved as if he'd been running like mad. "I have been looking all over for you! Please keep your hands off each other until the wedding. Please. I'm begging you. You are by far the worst couple I've ever had to chaperone!"

We stood like two children who'd been caught with their hands in the cookie jar. Brigham paced back and forth lecturing us about the proper behaviour of royalty and how we must act. Truthfully, I wasn't listening, I was staring at my daisy. I was so touched by his thoughtful gesture I could have kissed him.

Later that night, when the festivities were over and everyone was asleep, I stood in the garden staring at all the wondrous planets. I heard a sound behind me but wasn't scared. Turning, I saw it was Cade.

We said nothing but he came up to me slowly and his hands grabbed my waist pulling me close. He leaned in and I looked up accepting his embrace. His lips touched mine fervently and I welcomed it. Cade's hands slid down my back pulling me closer. Our lips parted.

"Cade," I sighed.

I jolted awake to someone grabbing me by the shoulder. It was Cade and he looked concerned.

"You were calling out for me." I *was*?! "Did you not sleep well last night?"

We were strapped into our seats and had long since taken off. I must've dozed at some point and felt flustered that I'd had such a passionate dream... about Cade.

"No. I slept well. Until it was interrupted when we got up at the butt-crack of dawn."

Cade's laugh escaped him like one who couldn't contain it and I became aware of our surroundings. Two high ranking officials sat in front of us listening to our every word. I felt my face heat up but to my relief the pilots at the front of the cabin stated we were now able to freely walk about the ship. I'd never unbuckled nor removed myself from a room so fast. My heart beat wildly in my chest. Cade saving a flower from Earth was incredibly sweet, so sweet in fact that I feared I was falling for him. Patting my cheeks, I splashed water in my face. "Focus, Jane," I said to myself. I didn't need the added distraction of Cade.

A knock sounded at the door. Drying off my face and taking a deep breath I opened it.

Cade stood waiting. "Hey, we'll arrive in Eirene soon and Lord Folke brought up an interesting point."

I followed him through the brightly lit ship towards a sitting area. Lord Folke and Lord Dwayne sat awaiting our arrival. Once seated, Lord Folke dove in.

"Miss Jane, we've been discussing a troublesome quarry. King Turton of the Eirenites is bent on defeating the Ares just as King Memign is of destroying the

Eirenites. After so much loss and war, both men have lost their humanity, so to speak. They are so determined to win they cut down anyone in their path."

Lord Dwayne interjected. "Our fear is if they discover that you are the would-be mother of the Ares, they would steal you and use you to build their own army. Strong enough to defeat the Ares once and for all."

Cade laid a protective hand over mine. "No matter. We shall conceal her identity. Introduce her as my fiancée and the only survivor of Earth."

I pulled my hand away. "Hang on. If they use me to build an army, doesn't that still accomplish our goal? We want to get rid of the Ares and if that's how we do it, I'm willing."

Lord Folke smiled. "A brave sentiment, but if the Eirenites win what will stop them from conquering other worlds, just as the Ares do now? Besides, we can't very well just give up our future queen like that."

"Do you mean to say we are taking out one foe and giving rise to another?" Cade asked. "Are these accusations grounded or merely speculation? It was always my understanding the Eirenites rose up to fight the Ares to keep them at bay when all others failed."

Lord Dwayne cleared his throat and avoided answering, just like a politician. "We are merely saying, sir, that with the Ares out of the way, there is nothing stopping the Eirenites from seizing power."

Cade rubbed his temples. "You didn't think of bringing this up at the ball?"

"King Edgarr was adamant. We hoped you would listen to reason."

I stood up, finished with this debate before it could truly start. "Gentlemen. Our present concern is the Ares. If the Eirenites suddenly lust for more power, is it the Almourrian's duty to police them?"

Lord Dwayne grew tight-lipped. "No," he ground out.

Lord Folke jumped in. "Of course not! But we don't want the Almourrian name besmirched. And we certainly don't want to be the lynchpin that creates a tyrannical Eirene empire."

I rolled my eyes. "Let's just attend the meeting and then discuss. Right now, we don't really have another option, do we?"

Neither men met my eye.

"That's what I thought. Now if you'll excuse me, I am going to take a nap. Wake me when we arrive."

Cade jumped up and held out his arm. "Let me escort you." It wasn't a question and I guessed he just wanted an excuse to leave.

"Sleep well. Don't dream of me."

I gasped but he swiftly shut the door before the pillow I threw could hit him.

I sat on my bed contemplating. I hadn't been having nightmares about my family anymore. My passionate dream of Cade was the first I could recall that wasn't even remotely connected to our war with the Ares. Maybe he didn't just make me feel safe, he invoked feelings within me that for too long I had been too scared to allow. After Luke, I'd shut off my heart but with Cade, it was like I couldn't suppress it. I was so drawn to him that I couldn't curb the feelings and that was scary. I knew in my heart of hearts he was nothing like Luke, but that didn't mean

Cade felt the same way about me. Was I doomed to a loveless marriage?

I threw myself on the bed, too frustrated to sleep. How could I be thinking about my love life at a time like this? I had to get my priorities straight. Whole worlds were burning around me.

CHAPTER TWENTY-FIVE

Eirene was colossal. I'd thought Almourr was big, but Eirene dwarfed Cade's home planet, simply putting mine to shame. Everything was metal; not a tree or flower of blade of grass was in sight. Huge towers reached the skies filled with hovering crafts and what looked like hot air balloons. It was staggering how many people walked about, each with their own purpose and destination. Our ship was docked and an Eirenite met with us to lead us to our rooms. Eirenites were peculiar to look at. Their skin was transparent and I could see their muscles contract when they walked, spoke, and even blinked. They were the size of humans and all lacked hair. It was very fascinating and all too distracting. I missed everything the man said.

"We wish to speak in the English tongue."

The Eirenite bowed and complied. It all sounded English to me. I supposed that chip in my brain was still working.

Once in our rooms, the man left. Cade, Brigham and I were in a suite with three bedrooms.

"On the morrow, you shall meet King Turton," said Brigham quite excitedly.

He still looked a little green from our trip. The entire time he'd been confined in his room and was ready for a nap. He looked like he was about to fall asleep standing up and I grabbed his arm to steady him.

"Brigham, you need to go rest."

He shook his head stubbornly. "No. You two need a proper chaperone." He could barely talk.

I folded my arms in front of my chest. "Believe me, nothing will happen." My eyes slid to Cade and his brows rose in complete innocence.

He put his right hand over his heart. "I swear we won't tell the king."

I puffed out a sigh. "Yes, because there won't *be* anything to tell."

I led Brigham to his room and once I saw him to bed, firmly shut the door.

Cade was on me in a second. "We have the whole day to explore. Care to join me?"

I couldn't even pretend to be angry. Explore another alien planet? It wasn't even a question. We donned plain clothes before heading out into the city. The sky had a strange purple hue and a brilliant white sun.

"Where are all the plants?" I asked, looking around.

Cade explained. "This planet is dead. Nothing can grow here. Those domes over there, do you see?" I followed the direction his finger was pointing and in the distance four great glass domes lined the horizon. "Those are green houses. They have to grow their food in there. They even have to ship in soil using teleportation."

"*Teleportation?*" I cried.

He looked at me like it was as ordinary as the hovering ships. I really shouldn't have been surprised. "Yes. Teleportation of inorganic matter."

"What about people?"

"There is a setting for that… But it isn't exactly stable."

I studied him, still adjusting to the idea that teleportation was a real thing and reverted back to our original topic. "Why is the planet dead?"

"The war began on Trireme, when it was still just a planet orbiting a sun. King Memign saw that his empire would be destroyed and began work on a ship so huge it was like another planet. When Trireme was inevitably destroyed, the Eirenites thought they'd won but then the remaining Ares fled to the ship, and it is what you see now, a vast empire ever growing. Perhaps even greater than before."

"This still doesn't answer my question."

"Right. The Ares brought the war here and it quickly became a dead planet. The Eirenites rebuilt and took the war to the stars where they still battle, even now."

Staring at all the magnificent architecture around me, I couldn't help but wonder: "How long has this war been going on?"

"Four hundred years I'd say. Both King Memign and King Turton have bred warriors to fight for them and that includes clones of themselves."

I shuddered. Every clone movie I'd ever seen ended badly, usually in war and death. Reality seemed no different.

We spent the day exploring, trying strange foods and even sneaking into the greenhouses.

"I've never seen this tree in person before!" exclaimed Cade as he inspected a tree whose roots grew upwards, getting its nutrients from the air and misty artificial rain. The roots soared above us in a network of intricately wound branches.

I picked up a seed off the ground. "You should take one home. For your garden."

Cade looked at the soil encrusted seed in my hand. "Alright," he whispered excitedly like it was the most forbidden thing he'd done in his life. Never mind we were currently trespassing.

That night I lay in bed staring up at the ceiling. Brigham claimed he was feeling much better at dinner and Cade had lied saying we'd stayed in the room the whole day. I didn't think Brigham believed him but he also didn't object.

The following day was a blur. Our small party was ushered into a towering room where twelve officials sat in raised chairs, at the head was King Turton. He was younger than I imagined and almost handsome, except that I could see his innards.

"Proceed," he loudly said.

Lord Folke stood and explained the situation, including the fall of Earth and Almourr's near annihilation.

King Turton pursed his lips. "What do we have to do with this? Are you complaining?" he roared.

"No, no my liege. Never. We are merely stating that Prince Cade and his fiancée were able to infiltrate Trireme last week but to take down King Memign and Queen Jezebel, we need further assistance."

"Do not speak those names to me! They are filth!" spat the king angrily. "I am more than willing to assist you, but our ships can hardly approach Trireme much less get on board."

"We are willing to lend you our fleet. The Almourrians are weak in number but you, my lord, have thousands on hand." Lord Folke displayed the utmost respect but King Turton seemed unperturbed.

"I do," he boasted. "But how can we know they won't recognize you after your little escapade last week? Besides, one small ship can go undetected, but thousands? Hardly. Those Ares aren't *that* stupid."

Lord Folke glanced back at Cade and I. A touch of worry lined his face. If the Eirenites didn't lend us aid, we were done for. The Ares would continue destroying planets and I didn't have to be a rocket scientist to know Almourr would be high on the list, given their association with me.

Cade abruptly stood. "King Turton. Forgive my rude behaviour but to be perfectly candid, this war has no feasible end in sight. Either act now or the Ares will continue to go behind your back, destroying planet after planet. You know what they search for, yes?"

King Turton shifted in his seat, clearly bored. "Yes. But the would-be mother does not exist! It's a fool's errand!"

"If you truly believe this how can you let them kill millions of people over nothing?" Cade clenched his fists in anger but kept his voice even.

I stood too, now, without thinking. It had to be said. Lord Folke and Lord Dwayne looked on in alarm as Cade took his seat to let me talk.

"The mother does exist. I am she!" It felt good to hear my voice reverberate off the metal walls and watch all twelve men clamour in alarm.

King Turton's eyes widened. "If what you say is true, girl, we must hide you from the Ares at all costs. They must never find you."

The twelve men began to shout angrily and all at once. "Where would be far enough?"

"We should kill her!"

"She could be our mother!"

"It's not safe for her to be here!"

"She is a threat to us all!"

Cade stood and grasped my arm. "Jane is my fiancée. Almourr takes responsibility for her!"

"Quiet!" ordered the king, subduing his council.

"My lord, I have an idea." I turned to Cade and whispered softly. "But you won't like it."

Sure enough, the king was satisfied while Cade's eyes grew dark and he vehemently protested.

CHAPTER TWENTY-SIX

Cade led me out of the Almourrian ship, my hands cuffed, and several weapons hidden well on his person.

"How did you even come up with this?" he whispered, still grumpy that everyone was allowing me to do this.

I shrugged. "I watched too much *Doctor Who.*"

Once again, Trireme loomed over us in all its Romanesque glory. Ares guards stood to our right and left and at the end of the line the king and queen gloated proudly.

"We're so pleased you've taken pre-emptive actions to save Almourr. In the new Ares Empire, we shall leave you and your people alone in peace."

Cade bowed graciously although King Memign was clearly lying.

My fingers twitched in anticipation. Hopefully, the king would lead me straight to the laboratory where I'd break free from my artificial cuffs and kill him, ending this war once and for all.

Meanwhile, I watched Cade's ship take off, leaving me behind; but I knew only Brigham was on board, as Cade had slipped away, ducking behind a large Ares ship before anyone noticed. When the moment was right, he'd slip into small cracks in the rock formations, just as we'd done the first time.

King Memign turned me around to face the Ares crowd.

"Our mother has arrived!"

Inspired shouts rang through the yard.

"She will birth the next generation of armies and we will defeat those pathetic Eirenites once and for all!"

The roars grew louder and I resisted the urge to cover my ears. Not quite knowing how I'd 'birth the next generation' had me feeling squeamish. Did he understand the anatomy of humans? Birthing a baby took time...lots of time. Not to mention how many he'd need to build an army.

The king shoved me none-too-gently towards the bowels of Trireme.

"I wish to delay the birthing process no further! Are the pods ready?"

A distinguished Ares stepped forward. He matched the king in height and wore blue robes embroidered in gold, I assumed it portrayed his rank as a scientist.

His eyes glowed with excitement. "Yes, my lord. But there is a shortage of power so the batteries need time to charge."

"How much time?" The king clipped.

"No more than twenty minutes."

"Fine. If it cannot be helped, we two shall dine in my study. She will need the energy, no?"

I was surprised at how reasonable he was being and the knot tightening my stomach lurched. The longer the king remained alive, the more our plan was put in jeopardy.

Helplessly, I obeyed the king's commands. The door shut and we were locked in his gaudy study, alone. Fear crept up inside me as I anxiously glanced about the room. There was no natural light in the room. Large golden chandeliers covered in dripping candles lit the spacious area. Books and ledgers were collecting dust on elaborately carved shelves and papers littered the desk where he obviously worked hard to run the country.

"Jane, feel at ease," he ordered. "You should feel honoured. Many have mothered the Ares armies but each generation has been a disappointment. But you... Your DNA is simply superb. I haven't seen anyone so compatible."

I rubbed my eye, triumphantly removing the fleck of dust and simultaneously ignoring him. King Memign pushed a large plate of what looked like food closer in front of me. "You will need your strength. Eat up."

I shoved the plate away childishly. "I'm not hungry."

"I take pleasure in how much pain you will endure this night."

"Will I survive?" I asked dully.

He tapped his fingers on the wooden table. "No. Once we have your DNA, replicating it will be easy. Unfortunately, we need *all* the DNA. And no one has survived the procedure."

"What will you do with it?"

"Replicate it and fuse it with Ares DNA, thus giving birth to an entire army of Ares. Once the pods are charged, we will proceed."

I fingered my axe, which was strapped firmly to my inner thigh. If I didn't succeed, Cade and the others would. They had to.

"Isn't it disgraceful that your armies are..." I searched for the correct words, "half-bloods? They're intermingled with me, a lowly human."

The king leaned forward. "Indeed. That is why we send them to war."

A knock sounded at the door interrupting the meal. King Memign stood and, grabbing my arm, raced to the laboratory.

It was a strange juxtaposition. The stone archways and pillars felt ancient but once I stepped through the wooden door, metal machines and glass vials lined the walls, some with strange glowing liquids. Instantly I was reminded of Almourrian plants. A glass chamber hummed with energy and I could only assume it was for my 'procedure'. A chair sat there ominously with heavy leather straps.

Queen Jezebel stood waiting for us. Her flowy crimson robes made her eyes glow like fiery orbs and her jet-black hair strung down to her ankles. She truly was grotesque.

She greeted the king sweetly and shot daggers at me with her eyes. "You," she pouted. "I understand you tried to escape." She scoffed. "A disgraceful coward you are. And ugly, too."

"Likewise," I shot back.

Hatred and anger simmered behind her yellow eyes. She drew near and I held my breath; for some reason I expected her to stink. "I will enjoy watching you suffer."

I shrugged, purposely looking bored. "So everyone keeps saying." I rolled my eyes. "Blow up one arena and everyone hates you," I muttered.

The queen backhanded me for my flippant comment. Reeling, I lay sprawled on the floor. Feigning unconsciousness, I used the opportunity to slowly uncuff myself and slip the axe from its safe hiding place. I couldn't move too fast or they would know, but move too slow and I'd miss my shot. My heart raced and listening intently, I waited as the king scolded his wife for her outrage and once the queen drew near enough again, I swung the freed axe with all my might. It met with two of her arms, sticking with a sickening display of blood and flesh. To my dismay, no golden light emitted from my blade as before and I looked on in confusion. The king looked smug as his wife cried out in pain. She wailed and crumpled to the ground clutching her bad arms.

"Yonan, explain."

Yonan, the white-robed scientist stepped forward. Obviously pleased with his moment to shine, he confidently obeyed his king. "The room is rigged with pulsamic sphygmos energy barriers. In short, your weapons won't work in this room."

"Energy barriers?" I repeated, feeling my heartrate pick up speed.

"Yes," The king interjected.

I glanced at the door.

"And you can try to escape," he continued, "but the door is bolted from the outside. I told you when we met, I gave you your powers, and I can take them away."

I didn't need to know the logistics, all I needed to know was my axe wouldn't work the way I initially thought. Throwing my billowy robes off me, I flung two daggers at Yonan, one to the neck and the other his eye. These weapons could slice Ares flesh and with satisfaction I watched him slump to the ground. But before the king or I could react, Queen Jezebel ran at me with a long blade screaming "You wretch!"

She blindly thrust her dagger she was so outraged. But her speed and height made it difficult to attack. She swatted at me with her cut arms and made contact. I fell to the ground hard. She moved to stab me in the face. Rolling out of the way in time I sliced her legs as I went and she stumbled to her knee. Ruthlessly grabbing her hair, I held my axe to her throat. King Memign had acquired a sword off the wall and now pointed it at me.

"Drop it!" he commanded.

I stared him in the eyes. Beneath me, Jezebel heaved angrily but became very still when my blade pierced her neck just the slightest, drawing blood.

I didn't expect fear to reflect in Memign's eyes and I was right; there was none. We were at a stalemate but, in the end, it wouldn't matter if I killed her. I wouldn't even put it past him to kill the queen himself in order to get to me. Think, Jane, think!

A banging sounded behind the barred door.

King Memign grew weary. "Leave us!" he shouted, but the banging persisted harder.

It was my turn to look smug. "Did you honestly think the Almourrian prince gave me up and just left?"

The king stood frozen in place, a cold frown hardening his features. Queen Jezebel attempted to swat at me but I in turn pulled her hair harder. She grunted and remained still.

"We went to the Eirenites and hatched a little plan."

The king paled at the mention of his enemy.

"Cade snuck aboard while you were distracted with me," I continued, "and planted four teleportation devices on your ship. As we speak, Eirenites are pouring through cutting everyone down."

"That's impossible! You're bluffing! Teleportation devices can't bring living creatures across."

I smiled. "They can if they're enhanced with a Faraday Cage." It was a metal cage that protected the living cells from the electric shocks and widened the teleportation range.

The king's hands shook with rage. I knew from spying the titles of his books that he was a learned man. "You…" his lips set together in a straight line.

I taunted. "It was easy really. If it wasn't for you telling me about Eirene, I never would have known." I smiled sweetly but the king looked murderous. Still he remained unmoving, fatuous in place.

The door suddenly burst open. Cade stumbled in and before he had time to assess the room, King Memign grabbed him, mirroring my own hold on the queen. "Let her go or he dies."

No. My heart nearly beat out of my chest. I didn't want this but what could I do? If I let Queen Jezebel live,

King Memign would still kill him. Then he'd use me and kill billions more. One life was not worth that many. Even if it was Cade's.

Everything around me slowed down and I stared between the king and Cade. We locked eyes. Cade said nothing, just barely nodded his head and shut his eyes. Accepting his fate. Somehow his understanding made it more painful. I could have come to love this man.

"I'm sorry." I whispered.

Jezebel tensed in anticipation of what she knew was to come. Stepping away from her with my hand still tangled in her mane I pulled exposing the neck and in one fluid movement, dislodged her head from the rest of her. I threw her dripping head at the king's feet. He stared silently, boiling rage simmering just below the surface. With a war cry he smashed Cade's body to the ground and lunged at me.

"Cade!" I cried, but he was lifeless.

I didn't have time to grieve as King Memign attacked ferociously. I had miscalculated; the king did care for his wife.

No words passed between us, just the clang of metal on metal as I blocked blow after blow. I was quickly losing strength and tried to assess how I could get the upper hand. The room was small with strange equipment. The axe grew heavy in my arms. I couldn't keep this up much longer. The king had me backed into a corner. As he raised his arms to strike again, I did a tuck-and-roll through his legs and tried to slice them as I'd done many times before. But I missed. He lunged again and, as I blocked another strike from his sword, his third arm landed in my gut. I doubled over gasping for breath. He kicked me hard in the ribs over and over. Picking me up, the king threw me at the wall. I crumpled to the ground coughing. The room was blurry. I was defenseless as he lifted me from the ground and slammed my body into the wall again. My feet couldn't touch the ground. One hand circled my neck and two pinned each arm which left one more to search my person for weapons. My grip on the axe loosened and my feet desperately tried to reach the floor. I squirmed under his touch but he didn't take pleasure in it. His yellow eyes were burning with rage.

Finding a blade, he traced it along my jaw before stabbing me in the side. A sadistic grin lifted the corners of his mouth. I gasped as the sting became potent. Leaving the blade stuck in my side he searched me for another. Upon finding one, and without hesitation, he stabbed my shoulder. I cried out despite myself and gritted my teeth to deal with the writhing pain. My vision blurred and hot blood poured down my shirt drenching my clothes. I gasped for breath. I almost couldn't feel the third blade, so tight was his grip around my neck.

"You killed her," he ground out.

Unable to think, I focused on trying to breathe, but he was blocking the airway. My lungs burned and the knives radiated pain over my torso.

"I'll beat them all!" he cried maniacally. Opening the glass door, he shoved me into the chair. Unable to resist he strapped me haphazardly into the seat.

"Please. Stop." My voice barely came above a whisper. My breathing was shallow.

"You deserve this!" His arm found my neck again and just as he found the fourth dagger, King Memign's discarded sword carved the arm gripping me clean off. Taken aback, the king recoiled and I slumped in the chair, wheezing, but even that effort felt like too much.

Cade stood above me, his forehead bloody and a cut on his arm but otherwise he seemed okay. The king found my axe and still clutched my dagger tightly in his grasp, ready to fight despite his wound. As air reached my lungs, I could only watch helplessly while the two clashed, sword to axe. The ring of metal was the only sound I could hear as they fought. I had to do something but try as I might moving seemed impossible. I was losing strength at an alarming rate. Willing my arms to move I was finally able to untangle myself from the straps in the chair. The king had been so angry he didn't confine me properly. I promptly fell to the ground in a heap.

The king threw my blade but Cade easily blocked the blow and rushed King Memign. The two got too close and powerlessly I watched the king dislodge Cade's weapon and, throwing my axe down, begin to hit Cade. Cade blocked and returned the punches but they weren't nearly as powerful as that of the nine-foot giant. I looked away from the gruesome sight.

"Jane!" Cade called and I looked to see him pointing at my axe then at a strange metal box with buzzing coils inside.

Mustering my strength I rolled and managed to reach the axe. I could do this. Repeating an encouraging mantra, I picked myself up off the floor and staggered toward the box. Hoping with all my might it was the pulsamic sphygmos energy barrier, I hacked the box to bits. The box was easily dismantled and sparks flew chaotically around the room. The vibrating coils increased in speed but then the box smashed to the ground and imploded. I slumped to my knees.

"Now!" called Cade.

I swung with all my might and a brilliant gold light burst across the room slicing the king's legs. An agonizing scream split the air as he fell on his back. Cade wasted no time in retrieving the sword and plunged it into King Memign's chest. He clawed desperately but soon the light drained from his eyes and his hands grew still.

Cade pulled the sword out of the king and flung it across the room. The king and queen were dead.

He rushed to me.

"I'm sorry," I gasped.

"No." He said firmly. "You did the right thing. Come."

He hoisted me to my feet and put an arm around my waist, the other held my hand around his neck.

"We have to hurry!" he urged. "I was late because I armed a planet killer. Its roots will reach the core in minutes!"

Leaving the axe and daggers, we picked up our speed. "I thought you said… that takes years."

"When they have to burrow through solid rock and soil, but this is a ship. Lots of open space."

Gathering all my strength I ran with him through the corridor. All around us Eirenites expertly battled the giant Ares. The clash of swords and agonizing screams sullied the air and the stench of blood dazed me. I blinked rapidly fighting to stay conscious. Losing strength, I sagged against him.

"Cade," I whispered.

A determined frown set his mouth. "We can do this. We just have to be sneaky and avoid a battle with any Ares."

I nodded and he tightened his grip around my waist.

Keeping to the shadows, we ran through the labyrinth of stone archways and luxurious gardens. Every curve brought the hope that we were at the shipping yard and each time was a disappointment.

"How much further?" I grunted as we stopped and waited for a clear path.

"Not far."

"We should have bandaged these before leaving."

"No time. The bomb will go in three minutes."

"Shouldn't we warn the Eirenites?"

Cade shook his head sadly. "King Turton was expressly clear. These war clones were not to return. Their job is to keep the Ares at bay. They know what they're doing. He said war-torn clones have no place in the free world."

Heaving me upright we ran through an empty archway.

I tried to argue with him over this matter. "We can't just leave them!"

Cade didn't reply and, as we rounded another bend, two Ares came running up. Both were armed with spears and hatred for the would-be mother who brought this havoc to Trireme. Cade set me down gently and caressed my cheek before leaping up a pillar and powerfully striking each guard with his sword. One fell to his death.

The other managed to block Cade with his spear. Cade jumped back to avoid being impaled and used his sword to push the spear lopsided, running close to the guard. I'd never seen him move so fast. With the claw dagger, he pierced the Ares's neck. He sputtered and flailed the spear wildly before tumbling beside his fallen mate. The spear nearly hit Cade in its wake. Hauling me to my feet, Cade practically carried me to the shipping yard. Brigham awaited us in the ship calling for us to hurry.

The pain in my side was subsiding and keeping my eyes open felt difficult. We jumped inside and Cade locked the door. The ship was in the air instantly.

Brigham ran over to us victoriously. "Have we won?" A huge smile warmed his face until he caught sight of me.

Cade carried me inside.

"We're going to get you cleaned up. Jane?"

I opened my eyes at the sound of my name.

"Wait. I want to see…."

Cade brought me to a window and in awe, I watched the bombs explode. Mushroom clouds made the sight nearly uneventful but when the implosion began, I could see Trireme burning. The pillars had crumbled to ash and the once splendorous planet was reduced to dust. Tiny bits of rock would be all that remained of King Memign's great empire. Satisfaction welled up inside me. Perhaps I should have felt remorse or sadness at so much loss, but I did not. I closed my eyes, finally feeling peaceful for the first time in almost three years. The sound of Cade desperately calling my name couldn't persuade me to open them and I drifted off to sleep.

CHAPTER TWENTY-SEVEN

I opened my eyes to a serene setting. Birds chirped overhead, the rustle of trees sounded in the gentle breeze and I was laying in bed with a mountain of pillows. I was once again on Almourr, in my bed. Turning to look outside I saw Cade standing, hands behind his back, staring over the waterfalls listlessly. His arm was bandaged and he looked tired. Slowly shifting to a more comfortable position proved hard work. The rustle of the blankets made Cade turn to me sharply. Running over to me, he bent down and, placing a hand on my neck, kissed me fiercely. Just as I was getting over the shock of it, he released me and stepped back.

Cade cleared his throat self-consciously. "Forgive me. I'm just glad you've woken up."

I sat up slowly, wincing at the pain everywhere and trying to process what just happened. "How long was I out? Did you drug me again?"

He chuckled. "No, Jane. You were out for three days. I have to tell everyone you're awake!" Abruptly he stood and left, no doubt avoiding the fact that he kissed me. A little bit of me was relieved. Was I okay with Cade kissing me?

The days passed into a solid month. The wedding had been postponed due to my injuries and it was the night before the big day. All the arrangements had been made, Everest and I had found a stunning gown and now I could only count the hours until we said 'I do'. If Almourrians did indeed say that…

My wounds were all healed, only bruises remained. Lying on my back, I stared up at the ceiling. Blossoms softly lit up my room and rain poured in heaps outside. The ceiling jutted out far enough that the water didn't pour into the room and I adored the sound of it so I lay there trying to fall asleep but to no avail. Hoping to reset my nighttime schedule, I eventually sat up opting for a glass of water.

On my way back from the trek to the kitchen I heard someone call my name. I held my breath and strained to hear.

"Jane!"

It sounded like Cade and following the sound, came to a hall that led me to his bedroom. Peeking inside I heard his bedsheets rustle and he called my name again. Cade was talking in his sleep and sounded distressed.

Creeping up I nudged his shoulder. "Cade?" I whispered. "I'm here."

He rolled over and in one fluid motion grabbed me and pinned me down on the bed, a claw dagger at my throat.

"Cade, it's me, Jane."

The dagger was immediately removed from my neck. "What are you doing crawling into my bed?"

"Crawling!? You grabbed me, you brute!" Shoving him off me, I began scrambling off the massive bed.

He laughed. "I was only teasing."

"You-"

"Cade?" Brigham's voice stopped me dead. If he were to come in now and see us like this we'd be done for, especially on the night before our wedding.

Cade pulled me off the bed in a flash. "You have to hide!" he whispered.

"Under the bed?" I quickly suggested.

"That's the first place he'll check!" he hissed.

"At least I'm making suggestions!"

"I have a better idea." Then, albeit my protesting, he shoved me outside into the pouring rain just as Brigham rounded the corner. I was drenched in moments but hid among the huge leaves of a nearby bush.

"Were you talking in your sleep?" I heard Brigham say.

Cade made a cheeky comment and soon, after more badgering, Brigham left. I waited a moment before emerging from my hiding place, anger keeping the cold at bay. I was in nothing but a thin short nightgown and the cloth stuck to my body making me feel very exposed. Heaving myself back into the room I glared up at him.

My teeth began chattering and my legs shook. "You *are* a brute," I muttered angrily. Water pooled at my feet and my hair was a sopping mess.

He chuckled and swept a big blanket around my shoulders, instantly warming me.

"Sorry but Brigham would have died on the spot had he seen us together in bed in the middle of the night."

I nodded; admittedly he was right. Still, he didn't have to shove me in the rain.

Looking up at him, my legs felt weak for a different reason. Cade was shirtless, his hair was a mess, and that adorable dimple fit snugly in the corner of his smile.

I took a step closer. "Thank you, Cade. For saving my life and stopping the Ares. All these weeks and I've never found the chance to say it."

"You're welcome. You know, I have something to tell you too." He leaned in close to whisper in my ear. His breath sent shivers down my back. "I actually do know what sexy means."

My face went crimson and an embarrassed gasp escaped my lips. I shoved him away and he fell backward right into the rainy forest. He was outside for but a moment and even still, he too was positively soaked.

I laughed despite myself and forgot my embarrassment.

Cade stole the blanket from me and wrapped himself up warmly. A shiver shot up my arms. "Hey, I wasn't done with that."

Smile gone from his mouth, he slowly unfolded his arms, and beckoned me forward. My legs moved on their own and suddenly his arms, wrapped in a blanket, were wrapped around me. With my chin on his chest I looked up at him and smiled. But then his eyes met mine and I blushed at being caught staring.

"Do you still think I'm sexy?" he asked quietly.

I stomped a foot trying to think of a clever way out. "Who's to say I thought you were sexy? I could barely see straight and it was dark. I was *very* delusional."

Cade smirked and caressed my cheek. "I've thought you were beautiful since I laid eyes on you." His finger traced my jaw. "And irresistible when you wore that dress for tea."

"Not before?" I asked, masking how much I just wanted to kiss him.

"This whole time it's been *very* difficult to keep my hands off you."

My heart was beating a mile a minute and still I opened my mouth to retort.

"Shut up," Cade whispered and bent close. His lips met mine. It was tender and questioning until I kissed him back. His hands travelled up my back pulling me close and taking my breath away. The blanket fell to the floor but neither of us felt cold.

That night, we sat by the window watching the rain. Holding hands, we talked about everything and although neither of us was ready to say those three little words, we both knew it would be short in coming.

"Ready to get married?" I asked.

The Beacon began blooming and its light spread over the city. Today marked the beginning of something new and wonderful.

"Of course."

Cade kissed me before shoving me outside lest Brigham catch us.

EPILOGUE

Cade came rushing into my office at an outrageous hour dripping in sweat and breathing hard. We had been married for three months and everything was going as smoothly as one might expect. Except Cade knew never to interrupt me when I was working. A month ago, I'd taken it upon myself to try and record human history and their inventions as best I could. I was obsessed with the work and tended to stay up too late working on it.

I swallowed my frustration though as this was clearly an emergency. "What's the matter?"

He smiled revealing the dimple. After all this time is still hadn't lost its charm. Cade paced the room back and forth seemingly too excited to form coherent words.

"It's about Earth."

I was all ears now. Earth was still an untouchable subject for me so I knew if Cade was bringing it up it was important. I willed my heart to stop beating so wildly.

"Cade, what is it?" I croaked.

He came near and grabbing my hands, led me from the room.

"They've just arrived! A Giatrosian and a human from Earth."

I stopped dead feeling faint. "What? How is this possible?" My voice barely reached a whisper.

"Come!"

In a daze I let my husband guide me to a comfortable sitting room where we usually met with more intimate guests. He sat me on the plush couch, handed me a glass of water, and plopped himself down beside me.

"They've only just arrived and I thought it best to let you know right away."

I nodded still speechless.

Cade frowned. "What's the matter? I thought you'd be more excited."

I glanced at him and set my glass down. "I want to be," I said trying to explain, "but I don't want to get my hopes up if this turns out to be some sort of hoax."

Before Cade could reply a woman and a man were announced. Asher, our butler, quietly shut the door behind them. His dishevelled state clearly meant Cade had roused him from sleep.

The two bowed awkwardly and we allowed them to sit.

It always fascinated me to watch Cade work. When he put on his kingly persona he was fair but very blunt. Not at all like his kind father, who'd passed two months ago. And very different from his usual flirtatious self.

The man, who was clearly not of Earth, with his cybernetic arm and medical tattoo, spoke first. "Thank you for speaking with us so soon. I am Chiron of the Giatros. This is Kate Wympery." Once formalities were exchanged, he continued, "we have heard of you and your husband's great feat of destroying the Ares. My thanks. We are here to deliver a message."

The girl, who looked as human as I, finally spoke. Her British accent was unmistakable. "I understand you tried to save Earth from the bomb."

I swallowed the lump in my throat. "Yes. We both did but alas, were unsuccessful. Earth perished."

Kate smiled and leaned in. "Earth did, yes, but all the humans were saved. They're all alive!"

I allowed myself to believe her. The weight of Earth's annihilation had been pressing on me and it was now suddenly gone. My heartrate picked up speed and a smile that I couldn't stop spread across my face. I leaned in as well. "Please. Tell me more."

The End

CPSIA information can be obtained
at www.ICGtesting.com
Printed in the USA
LVHW042229260719
625551LV00002B/6